I0891672

CARLY RACKLIN

FUNERAL SONG

DEAD SKY PUBLISHING

Paperback ISBN: 9781639512294

eBook ISBN: 9781639512430

Published by Dead Sky Publishing, LLC

Miami Beach, Florida

www.deadskypublishing.com

Cover by Alex Eckman-Lawn

Design & Formatting by Apparatus Revolution, LLC

Edited by Anna Kubik

Copyedited by Jenn Proffitt

For all those whose grief feels too monstrous to hold and too precious to put down

AUTHOR'S NOTE

Funeral Song is an in-depth exploration of grief, death, ritual, and mourning. It contains scenes of violence (including violence from a spouse), drowning, organized religion, body horror, gore, and discussions of war, death of a parent, and abandonment by a parent.

Thank you for reading.

PROLOGUE

Friede tried to scream, but no sound came out.

She blinked open grit-glued eyes, lungs spasming, until a jet of water seethed out from between her locked teeth. It spattered onto the floor with an echo so loud she thought her skull had shattered.

In cold, aching pieces, Friede's world coalesced into legibility.

The gray web of her lace shawl was snarled around her shoulders and arms, pinning her like a caught fish. She coughed, and more water splashed into the face of the broad figure crouched over her, holding her upright, their chest flush and shuddering against hers. Her mouth tasted like mud, teeth slimed with weeds.

She still felt hands clasped around her throat, but there was nothing there now. Just a memory, rising to the surface with bloat.

Friede coughed again, hard enough her bones creaked, and finally dislodged a stubborn cake of muck and more black water. Then she screamed.

The figure above her sobbed. He made short, birdlike keens between the tears that dripped from the tip of his wide nose onto her cheek. Something about those shining brown eyes of his unspooled a taut thread inside her. Damp curls curtained his eyes, and she wanted, instinctively, to brush them aside and look him full in the face, sure she would be warm again if she did.

"Bastian?" she croaked.

The sobs cut away with a sharp gasp. Then slowly, as if it hurt, he smiled. It was so lovely, and warm, and sad a look that Friede felt as if she was drowning all over again, rigor mortis clamping a possessive hand on her lungs.

She tried to remember what came before this, to follow those immaterial hands locked around her throat to a source, but like gazing into a dark, rippling pool, she beheld nothing. She remembered only pain, panic, and animal terror. The kind from nightmares, indistinct but omnipresent, pricking at every thread of her consciousness and spreading out into boggy dimness.

In every direction, that darkness. A bottomless cold.

Those hands, tightening.

She jerked in Bastian's arms, fighting restraint. Past the edges of her sodden nightgown, her reflection stared owlishly from a constellation of slow-blooming puddles, hair and eyes turned white as bleached bone. Another scream bubbled on the back of her throat and froze on her tongue. Friede choked it down, struggling for words instead.

The only ones she could dredge up were no, no, no.

"You're all right," said Bast, gently swiping the muddy hair from her face with cold hands.

He should have been warm. Why wasn't he warm?

His breath clouded the air before her with thick plumes, but she couldn't feel it, only his pulse drumming hard through their flush chests. A beat she couldn't keep. There was nothing left in her but cold.

"You're back," he whispered, giddy.

Friede shrank away from the words. But she was caught in Bastian's arms, caught in her body, caught under the sapping weight of water and truth.

It was her turn to sob, then, though no tears answered the call. She had only that quiet litany. *No, no, no.*

Try as she might to wish away the thought, there was no mistaking the dark, cold place she'd come from. Just as there was no mistaking the musty corridor she lay in now, where candlelight cast into stark relief scores of bones nestled neatly in alcoves. Thousands upon thousands keeping silent vigil.

Resurrection was the only reason the dead came to these catacombs in this age.

Friede fought to peer around Bastian. The comfort she'd found in the high ridge of his shoulders had soured; now it was one more layer keeping her cloistered, bound. Moving her neck was like rolling a heavy stone, but as she heaved it aside, she noticed for the first time the second figure tucked into the gloom.

Eluned, the Anchoret, held Death's skull between two wrinkled hands. Though pallid from years of confinement, her skin still held the telltale flush of life. In sharp contrast, the hallowed bone of the skull could have been a shard of obsidian carved from the night itself.

When Friede met her gaze, the other woman swept the skull into its shroud and turned away, retreating into a dim doorway as if bashful of the attention. Or perhaps ashamed. Could she sense Friede's pain as Death worked through her to wrestle her soul back to form? Did she even care whether she wanted to return or not? Or was she perhaps just as much of an unwilling vessel?

Friede tried to cry out after her, but her crushed throat forbade words. Was this part of Death's exchange? Her voice for her soul? She shuddered violently at the thought. She'd had no say in the bargain.

Bastian didn't appear to notice her struggle. He pressed his forehead to hers, still weeping, his smile now the sole beacon in the dark.

"Thank you, merciful Death, thank you," he whispered. The cold, clouded words fell over her like snow.

Hands immobile, Friede leaned harder against him, willing him to look at her, but he wouldn't. He rocked to and fro slowly, eyes shut in reverence, until their bodies were veiled in the thin fog of his soft-uttered prayers. "Praise All-Eternal-Death who restores life to the dead. Praise All-Eternal-Death who restores life to the dead ..."

Friede stared past him into the dark and waited for tears that refused to come.

CHAPTER ONE

AN INTERRUPTION

A light rain gauzed the air on the morning of Allhallowsmas, and through tall glass windows it cast the interior of the bone-church a moldering greenish-gray. The stormy sky sickened all the shadows inside the nave. Friede sat straight-backed at the grand piano, caged in the brightest spot on the floor to be found, though still too strangled to be called light.

She kept her gaze fixed on the head cleric, poised for her cue. Flexing her fingers against the creeping cold, she tried and failed not to think of the dank corridor of her resurrection, separated from her by only a few meters of stone floor below her feet, and only a handful of months. She was as aware of that time as she was of the rigid links of bone and tendon that strung together her hands where they dangled above the keys, eager to be put to work.

Rector Volf shivered behind the pulpit. His simple black uniform was too old and weathered to fend off Cairney's chill any longer, but the priest — older and equally weathered — refused to requisition a new one for the decades Friede had known him.

Their eyes met. Volf sniffed loudly and nodded. Friede brought her blue fingers to the keys.

The first few notes were always the sweetest; their thrum cut through the constant low murmur of water trapped between her ears, down to the bone. She danced her fingertips across the piano's ivory teeth as if feeding herself piecemeal to the keys, letting the melody luxuriate until not a shred of quiet remained. Until she could forget for just a little while what she had become.

She wasn't alone in her reverie. Music was beloved, especially to the dead. The vibrations of a viola's strings could bring phantom warmth to bloodless fingers. A swelling crescendo, caught at just the right moment, mimicked a heartbeat in the chest. A cello's low rasp filled one's throat like breath. All things the living savored and the dead craved — mourned, even. Although none would ever admit to the blasphemy.

Only when Volf looked on the verge of lapsing into sleep standing up did Friede relent. The last notes of the requiem rang from the ossified walls up to the arches with their glut of cobwebs, lingering so long in the air they seemed to almost gain form and encrust the congregants like frost.

Some dramatics were to be expected, today of all days. The thinning of the veil was palpable in the air.

When silence finally shrouded the small congregation, Friede took advantage of the brief interlude to study the dead man.

Julius Delvin was the most colorful thing in the room by far. A few weeks ago, he'd retired from his position teaching arithmetic to children and adolescents in the wind-chafed schoolhouse where Friede taught music, though death had forced her on sabbatical. Now he reclined on a long stone slab, crowded by snowdrops and wearing a creased yellow vest that must not have seen the outside of a wardrobe for some time. It was tucked and fastened in several places, but Friede could tell it had been tailored for a much broader man. She'd certainly never seen him wear it in life. Usually, the dead were clad in plain white shrouds for funerals, but his family must have insisted, for appearance's sake. Friede was glad for the brightness.

But despite the finery he'd been swaddled in, Mr. Delvin's brows were ever so slightly pinched, like the business of dying was all very inconvenient for him. Like he'd rather be anywhere else. Friede sympathized.

However you cut it, dying was often inconvenient. An interruption. Schedules had to be amended, arrangements made, and family pulled from their own important business. But tradition was tradition, and no tradition was more important than that which had been handed down by the Angel of Death themselves. Life in Cairney subsisted on it, depended on it. Day after day, interruption after interruption.

Today's affair was a small one. Immediate relatives only, the usual production and rapid turnaround to ensure the most optimal resurrected state — but still enough for a family of decent public standing to appear respectable, fastidious in their devotion. Friede played her part, the same one she'd chosen long before joining the ranks of Cairney's living dead. She liked to think it was the music, not the prayers nor Death's silent sneering skull, that truly enticed the souls back to flesh.

The Angel of Death's cold kiss woke them, but Friede was their herald. The dead were happy to see her when they woke, happy to hear her play. That line of thinking made the constant processions more bearable.

Friede's death had broken tradition. There had been no funeral or music to ease her sudden return to the world. After Bastian dredged her from the lake behind her house and carried her through the snow to the church, the body her soul had been stitched back into no longer fit quite right, like a garment shrunken from overwashing. Resurrection was an art, but an imperfect one. Factors like time and the manner of death meant one's new existence might not resemble their previous one very much at all.

Two months ago, Friede had been lithe and nimble. Two months ago, she'd been happy, with a loving wife, who, as far as she'd known, had never wanted to hurt her. Now her throat was bruised wine-red, and Lor was gone to the four winds. The stale tang of regurgitated water clung to her tongue and she wallowed about as if always caught in stubborn, sodden layers, a sinking weight ever stuck to her limbs. Her blood no longer moved; she had no breath, no warmth, no taste, no rest. And yet every other person in this room, living or dead, would still call it a miracle.

Friede stood from the piano. She couldn't take a heartening breath, but she could will her spine tall, her chest proud. She could pretend well enough to keep hold of the small ledge of content she'd scrounged from the fallow field that was her old life. Anyone who spurned Death's blessings would never be welcome to assist in a funeral. There was no room in this sanctuary for grief.

The only one she couldn't fool was Bastian. Friede found her seat in the front pew beside him, fist tight on her cane as she went. His head was bowed, lips moving in prayer, though Volf hadn't started the proper rites yet. Between the blustering wind and rain tapping staccato on the windows, Friede barely caught the words, but recognized them easily, the same refrain etched in the stone plinth Julius Delvin rested upon.

Praise All-Eternal-Death who restores life to the dead.

She bit down on her cheek, wishing she hadn't listened at all, and drew her gaze from his mumbling lips to his soft jaw, tripping over the white sliver of skull peeking from the hollowed spot where his nose had sat until recently.

Bastian had found his own death only weeks ago, a face-down tumble into the rocky riverbed, gin bottle in hand. She ached picturing him that way, and avoided it as often as possible. He looked more peaceful now in death than he had for most of his life. That was a small comfort. Friede was glad for the moment that he was too occupied to look at her. She worried he might see her bald, bitter envy.

A few rows back, the pews creaked. Friede glanced over to find several stern, pinched faces staring ahead at the slab. Sisters, most likely; she guessed Delvin's. She liked the look of them.

Since nobody else would, Friede mourned for the dead man.

No one had mentioned to her what he'd died from, but it didn't appear to have been particularly gruesome. He still had all ten fingers, all limbs; his complexion was even if a bit dull. Hair still clung to his head and cheeks in thick charcoal-gray tufts. Natural causes, then. But simply because something was natural didn't mean it couldn't be horrible.

With or without a second life, death was loathsome — even the most natural, painless death, the quickest return. Lor had helped her understand that.

Friede treasured the blasphemous thought.

Settling into her seat, she shut her eyes as Volf began to pray. She knew the words, had them memorized as well as the clerics.

Sleeper, wake
Great-Winged-Death hears and sees you
This day and every day forevermore
Here you are offered a death without sorrow
Be at peace, for the merciful one beyond
All human name and order grants you rebirth
Never must you mourn for in love there is no end
Wake, sleeper
Wake.

The last few words sent a sourceless tremor up Friede's throat. She jerked in her seat, fists clenched on instinct.

Desperate for distraction, she listened for the telltale squeak of the wooden doors that spelled the entrance of the Anchoret with Death's skull to complete the rites. Eluned's ingress was usually silent otherwise, to keep everyone focused on the rites. But the church was a stubborn old thing, bloated with damp. Its hinges groused and groaned at every opportunity.

And yet, Friede heard only the wind singing against bone.

She squinted curiously around the room. The doors stood silent and firmly shut.

The wrongness of it ensnared all her attention in an instant. The

Anchoret was never late for the rites. Timing was part of the tradition. And tradition, like Death, was everything.

Volf continued, perfunctorily, "Sleeper, wake."

"*Wake*," whispered the room in one voice. Friede's jaw locked; she couldn't even mouth the words.

Still, the doors were silent. Still, no Anchoret.

Eluned was an old woman after all, edging on a century. Maybe she was having some trouble with the stairs. Maybe she needed help. Friede often did.

Friede's hand sought out Bast's. He startled, but leaned into the touch, brow quirked.

He took in the trouble a moment before the rest of the room did. Friede could practically hear Volf's brow furrow from the pulpit. The two men locked eyes, and by the time the first murmur started up, Bast stood sharply from the pew.

His face smooth, he would seem the perfect picture of a cool-headed cleric-in-training to anyone who hadn't known him since boyhood. But he'd learned his poker face from Friede. His smart mouth had gotten him into trouble often in their schoolyard days; though he could never quite manage to hold his tongue, she'd at least helped him stop wearing his intentions so baldly. Now his mouth was honest, even if his face was not.

Her worry only grew, like snow buckling a rooftop. The nave seemed to narrow around her. Dread brought the taste of river water up from her lungs. A sour wrongness, impossible to ignore.

Bast smoothed down the front of his robe. Where Volf's hung off his wiry frame, Bast's was a roughly hemmed handmedown, and hugged him tight across a round stomach and shoulders.

He turned and said only, "I'll be just a minute." His smooth half-smile might have pleased the room, but Friede saw its nervous cracks.

He could only be headed for the catacombs to see what delayed Eluned, but Friede stopped him cold with a glance. The least they owed her was keeping her informed. She wasn't a cleric, but she was just as key to a Cairney funeral as they were. And she'd spent more time with Eluned than either of them, seeking counsel, comfort, even confession sometimes, since her death. Eluned was more than a morbid skull-bearer. She was a friend now, too.

"Let me," Friede said, poker face firmly rooted. "You're going to make everyone worry, storming out looking like that."

A flash of mischief warmed his bronze eyes. He ducked to her level, smirking slightly. "Oh, how do I look?"

Friede resisted the urge to roll her eyes. A matching smirk tugged at the corners of her mouth. Had she always crumbled for him so easily? "Like you just pulled your favorite socks from the river." She nudged his arm. "Stay with Volf. Light some candles or something."

He gave her a true smile this time. "As if you don't look just as gloomy."

The pew gave a perilous squeak as she lurched up. She ignored the few stares it earned. "Nothing out of the ordinary, then. I've seen your frowns spark the stirrings of an angry mob."

He laughed. Volf cleared his throat from the pulpit a moment before footsteps clacked assuredly up the floor at their backs. Friede turned to see the throng of stern-faced sisters, all equally ashen, and knew the time had come to be scarce. She took the long way around to exit the pew, then the nave, the old hinges growling after her.

The pale corridor beyond held a different kind of quiet than the sanctuary. More alive somehow despite its emptiness. Sporadic voices and footsteps from elsewhere in the church trickled from the arches and between the cracks in stone, a prelude of the rush to prepare for the Allhallowsmas festivities beginning at sundown. Paper garlands in the shape of skulls adorned the sconces. Soon, snowdrop petals would run the length of every hall, a reminder of what grew from the blood-drenched earth after the northern war carved through Cairney generations ago.

Friede took just a moment to drink in the stillness before continuing down the hall. The thought of Bast fending off questions while Volf stammered through another set of prayers quickened her steps. She turned the corner and came to the tall black door leading down to the catacombs, another image of a skull greeting her at eye level, carved into the door's obsidian face.

She'd been dead and lost in the dark the first time she passed this threshold, and ever since, some part of her intuitively cowered before it. Her previous trips down to counsel with Eluned did nothing to dampen the soul-deep instinct that accosted her at the threshold. Trembling slightly, she fit her fingers into the hollows of the carved skull and pried the door open. It bore no lock. The hinges barely gave a whisper as she eased its bulk across the floor. Darkness pooled below.

Who'd let the candles go out?

There was only one real answer, but Friede didn't want to believe it.

She left the door ajar to let light in as she descended. The stairs were steep and narrow, with no hand rail, and she wondered how Bastian had managed to carry her corpse the long way down without falling to his death there and then.

Friede remembered the fear she'd felt upon waking like the echo of an injury. Every time she gazed upon the rows and rows of bones set into the walls, the scores lost to mortar and musket and malice, it stirred a seed of jealousy in Friede.

It was an ugly thought, but inescapable. That longing was woven into her despite how she hated herself for it.

These still and lifeless bones were casualties of unfathomable cruelty, two-thirds of Cairney's already emaciated original population. They had prayed and prayed for mercy even as the slaughter came down. The lucky survivors prayed until Death had heard them, so the story said. Shamefully glutted from war or perhaps just moved to pity, Death had given them the option of rebirth.

A curse disguised as a blessing, if you asked Friede.

The only tolerable thing about resurrection were those first few moments when Friede hadn't remembered she'd been murdered. That hadn't lasted long.

The haze had cleared, and now Friede knew that the hands

marked into her throat had belonged to Lor, her wife, and nothing would ever remove the knife of that knowing from her heart. She tried harder every day to forget. And every day, the knife twisted deeper, the wounds written in her flesh.

Neither could she forget these catacombs, and Bast's weeping — weeping Friede herself would never be able to express herself for what she'd lost. Everyone she encountered since then insinuated she should be thankful. Yet not one of them ever stopped to ask if this was what she'd wanted anyway.

It wasn't, of course. It was Cairney's dream. Not hers. Never hers.

That felt easier to think here, in the dark, among thousands who also hadn't been given a choice in the matter. At least these old bones wouldn't tell her secret.

Eluned wouldn't either; she'd promised as much the first time Friede came to her after her resurrection. That was the reason she kept coming back.

She took a moment to brace herself against the wall of skeletons, throat throbbing in memory. The hallway was a straight shot here, about the same length as the nave, but it felt longer, as if she might never reach the end of it.

The darkness turned on her then. The dark and the cold both, colder than usual. Cold like black water weighing her down.

"Eluned?" she called.

The sound was weak, but enough to dampen the rush in her ears for a moment. No answer came except a ragged echo. Friede tottered as fast as she could down the length of the hall, fumbling for matches and lighting the sconces as she went, past alcoves bursting with disarticulated dead.

Did they envy her in kind? Or would they too balk at her ungratefulness?

She meant to knock lightly on Eluned's door, but her hand shook too greatly for gentleness. The sound rattled her bones.

For a moment, she was terrified to open it, and equally terrified to turn back. What would happen if she were to see Death's fleshless face again? Everyone in Cairney told a different tale of how many eye sockets that skull held, what horror one would see if they looked upon it unshrouded outside of the proper time. Weeping blood, sudden blindness, instant fathomless death.

"There's a funeral on upstairs," Friede said, jaw tense. "You're needed."

I need you. I need to get out of here.

"Eluned?"

Beyond the thin door, wind hissed a gentle song.

"Oh, damn it." Friede pushed her way in.

Light fell onto the alcove where Death's skull should have sat. The white veil meant to shroud it from sight was absent, leaving a yawning emptiness behind. The one small window was broken and let in a spray of icy rain.

Eluned lay in her bed. Her gray-gold hair cascaded down to the floor; she was stained crimson from mouth to breast, the front of her plain white robes dark and dripping. Bloody vessels webbed over her vacant eyes. Her mouth hung open wide, painfully wide, lips locked in a scream no one had noticed.

Or perhaps she hadn't had the chance to scream.

Friede started immediately for her side, but her legs folded as if they were made of felt. She landed on her knees a few paces from the bed. Just close enough to see the purpling imprint of hands around Eluned's neck.

CHAPTER TWO

FATES WORSE THAN DEATH

Friede sat on a dusty stack of books in the corner of Volf's office, knees bent almost to her ears, a cup of tea with honey clasped between her shuddering hands. An utterly useless benediction. Drinking it would do her no good. Her throat had cramped from screaming anyway. The cords of muscle behind her tongue felt like bowstrings frayed to snapping.

Who had coaxed her up the stairs? Who had sent the congregation away? She tried to remember the blur of moments between now and when she'd found Eluned, mouth gaping and covered in blood, but she couldn't sort the pieces as they roiled in her head.

She was too focused on the return of those ghostly hands wrapped around her own throat. Just the same as those she'd seen bruised into Eluned's dead flesh.

Dead. Eluned was dead.

They'd spoken only last week, Friede offering wry updates on the goings-on in town. She tried to remember the rasp of Eluned's laugh after she'd relayed a bit of schoolhouse gossip, but the sound was poisoned by the screams Friede couldn't help but conjure from her corpse's slack mouth.

Would she ever hear that laugh again? Or massage the blood back into the old woman's cold fingers with her own? The only time Friede felt strong these days was when she helped Eluned up and down the stairs. Who would join with her in lamenting now? Bast suffered her griping with a smile, but Eluned gave as good as she got.

A loud and thankless part of Friede was furious at her for dying. Even near one hundred, she'd had more life in her than most in Cairney.

And they couldn't bring her back, because the fucking skull was gone too.

How? *When*? It didn't make any sense.

She'd always listened to Friede. But when it mattered most, Friede hadn't heard her.

Why hadn't she heard her scream?

Footsteps hissed over dust beside her. Someone had come, sat like a second shadow just out of range of her narrowed vision. They weren't touching — if anyone's hands came near her right now, Friede thought she might start screaming again and never stop.

The hands on her throat clamped tighter, tighter.

Friede made the mistake of staring at her reflection in the tea. She saw herself distorted and breathless under dark water.

She saw Eluned there too, just below.

Her whole body flinched, hands clenching. The cup shattered.

It hardly mattered; she couldn't feel the burn.

The figure beside her swore quietly — she knew it was Bast now by the way he dampened the consonants at the end of his softly uttered "*fuck*" — and began a valiant effort to clean up amid the mess that was Volf's office. His gaze bored into her, but Friede was wintered over, hunched and frozen inside herself. She waited for the world to come back into clarity, but it was frozen too, still fixed around her in pieces she barely recognized.

The room was likewise in disarray. She took in the fragments to keep from picturing Eluned again: the dining table and chair serving as a desk, the single bookcase that held mostly scattered papers, a collection of teacups (now minus one), a pot of leggy ivy reaching for the window. Somehow, Volf found enough bare space on the floor to pace back and forth, which he'd been doing incessantly for the last several minutes, moving with the weight of a metronome. Friede rocked to his steady cadence.

Outside, the rain had turned to hail, pellets ticking a tachycardic rhythm on the glass.

As Bast returned to his seat in the corner, the two clerics narrowly avoided colliding in a flurry of limbs. Volf's dark skin had turned ashy to match his receding hair, so wan Friede was tempted to think him dead. He'd always been a nervous man. Waspish and uptight as well, but he'd never winced in the face of death. No corpse had ever turned him this sickly shade, not in all the years Friede had been playing requiems.

But then, no corpse had ever been the Anchoret before.

She was Death's chosen keeper; Cairney was hallowed only as long as Death's skull remained within the church walls under her watch. She had taken her vow young and held the position longer than any other before her. She was as woven into the fabric of Cairney as the bones in the church walls. There was no Allhallowsmas without her to bear the skull and call Shepherd-Death down. Just the veil unstitched, a yawning mouth to cruel oblivion, ready to swallow all their souls up.

"Fuck," Friede whispered, shivering.

Had someone truly killed Eluned while the rest of them prayed just upstairs? Or had she been dead all morning, her soul lost in the dark and praying for their help, just as Friede had been? Stuck between here and the hereafter. The thought sickened her. And she didn't have the skill to read death's timing on a corpse; she knew nothing, nothing that could help.

Death was a state, a place, not just a moment. Like her melodies, it had become muscle-memory — the sensation of Lor's hands around her throat, lungs full of frigid water, trapped just inches below the world she knew but unable to cry out. Supposedly, she'd been dead for only an hour or two when Bast found her in the wee hours of the morning. Only a day after her and Lor's wedding. But Friede insisted that the horrible in-between had lasted longer than some odd hours. She could have been there for days.

No one belonged there. Certainly not Eluned.

The room started to blur again. Friede put her head into her hands, leaning on her knees.

At the same moment, Volf sprang up straight and stopped his restless circuit. He whirled around, the fine leather of his shoes squealing as he did.

"I think I might know — what if — that is ..." He wrung his hands, fiddling with a ring set with a small bone from some old martyr or other. Bast wore a similar piece. "Brother Ruz," he eventually settled on, "were all the young wards accounted for this morning?"

Bast cocked his head and took a beat to answer. "Actually, no. One bed was—"

"Kamil Kant was absent, yes?"

Friede didn't think she recognized the name, but she had little knowledge of the church activities outside of funerals and the occasional piano lesson. The shelter was on the other end from the sanctuary, a newer, better insulated addition, fitted with a kitchen, nursery, beds, supplies — a place suited for the living.

Bast nodded. "That's right. They probably ran off again. But there's no way they had anything to do with this."

"I've heard tales of Mx. Kant's sticky fingers." Volf didn't quite put his full breath into the accusation, but he didn't have to. He'd never excelled at subtlety.

The air turned charged as Bast straightened up, a sharp frown creasing his face. He shook his head decisively. Friede could almost hear the knife of it coming down.

"Those are lies. I've spent a bit of time with Kamil. They collect cast-offs from around town, but they're not a thief, and definitely not violent. Just lonely. They don't get along with the others because they're older."

"Indeed, Kamil Kant is old enough to know how unbecoming of a young adult it is to live off the charity of this institution while disregarding our rules, wouldn't you agree, brother Ruz?" Volf sat daintily behind the desk. A moment later, as if shaking off the scorch of Bast's gaze, he stood again. "Let us still locate them. Perhaps they heard or saw something if they were wandering about, flouting curfew yet again. Though I suspect they'll return for meals, as always."

"I'll check the apartment," Bast said, his jaw and fists tense. He fingered his buttons for a moment and stood, angling himself awkwardly so as not to knock anything over. Volf nodded and moved to sit back at his desk as if the conversation was done and dusted.

"What about Eluned?" Friede broke in. Her throat strained against the words, cracking them like Volf's porcelain.

Volf's mouth fell open as if surprised to find her still in the room. He swallowed loudly. "The Anchoret would want us to locate the skull immediately. Once it is returned, I will perform the rites, and all will be well again."

You can't even be bothered to say her fucking name, she almost said, but reined herself in at the last moment. She felt steaming and clumsy with so much anger.

She replied, "You make it sound so simple. Like a murder is no different from a shirt in need of ironing."

Sympathy muddied Volf's gaze, clouding over his nervousness. "It is a tragedy, Miss Inkerman, no doubt. But as you well know, we have Death's blessing, so we may be free of mourning for her."

Friede scoffed. *A tragedy*. What did that make her then, so pointedly not free of her mourning? Not for Eluned, and certainly not for herself.

She heaved to her feet. She stood inches taller than both men, though the height only made her dizzy now. Her hand drifted to her throat, where bruises so similar to Eluned's lay beneath her high collar. Evidence of a crime that would never fade.

Death broke one's heart a thousand ways, even once it stopped beating. Volf didn't understand; he wouldn't until his own body was stiff and bloodless and he woke in white on the nave's cold plinth.

"Did Death free you of a conscience, too, rector? What a balm your ignorance must be," she said, clasping her hands into fists.

If they didn't care to find justice for Eluned, she'd do it herself.

Her legs wavered traitorously, but they carried her to the door. She pushed herself through. By the time she reached the church exit, she was almost jogging, desperate to be free of all the colorless walls and bones sepulchered in stone. Even if she couldn't breathe it in, the harsh wintry air might wash some of the horror from her head if she steeped in it long enough. It couldn't hurt, at least. Nothing much could, anymore.

Friede burst through the doors into a blinding white horizon, slowing to a stop at the peak of the hill, her heels kicking up a trail of downy snow. The vastness overwhelmed her. All of Cairney was visible from the ridge where the church hunched, sliced clean into halves by the river's winding smile. Its edges blurred into birchwood for as far as the eye could see. She wished more than anything to take a breath of the bracing air, to feel the bite of the snow on her face.

From this angle, all the rooftops looked like snow-capped headstones. Winter was settled in snugly, and would stay that way for ten or so months before they ever saw the grass grow again. Friede knew the feeling, locked in a frigid shell of her own. The lighter layers of snow would be gone by high noon, leaving puddles in the lanes for children to kick through as school let out.

Friede flinched at the sound of those puddles now. Every joyous splish-splash was the perfect echo of her head dunking under the lake. She stared at her hands, tracing the discolored skin where her engagement ring had sat for a few blissful weeks, an heirloom from Lor's family, the only one to survive the war. She'd cast it into the river from this very spot after leaving the catacombs, while lake water froze on her face like the tears she couldn't shed. She was still cold. She would never not be cold.

Unless, an icy voice prompted from within.

Unless she took her leave tonight.

Volf had been needling, but Friede did know Death, and their so-called blessings. They'd offered Cairney two gifts when they first unfurled their black wings over the town. Rebirth, or eternal rest. It was easy to forget amidst the monotony of endless funerals and resurrections, but she still had a choice left.

When the sun sank into its own grave and Great-Winged-Death again descended on Cairney, dragging the dark behind them, she could run into their arms instead of away.

Her parents had done it. Signed the papers, made their arrangements. They'd known better, even if the ache of their absence still throbbed in Friede year after year. She could spurn Cairney's cruel indifference once and for all. Tonight, the veil would come unstitched, and Death would meet them atop this very hill to take their skull from the hands of the Anchoret, and —

No.

Eluned's contorted face surfaced from her memory.

No, none of that would happen.

Not with Eluned dead. Not with the skull missing.

The fragile hope inside Friede buckled, buried in an avalanche of dread.

She was as trapped as she'd ever been.

Friede's limbs locked. The world had turned wrong-side-up again. The sky glaring down was the color of Eluned's dead face.

She should tell Bast; they had to do something. Hail blotting at her cheeks and eyes, Friede turned back just as the church doors creaked open and Bastian stepped out as if knowing he'd been summoned. This time, he didn't bother with the poker face.

She glanced away at once, resolve melting.

"Well," he said, "that was ... tense."

"You mean dramatic. It was, wasn't it?" Friede couldn't staunch the satisfaction in her voice. "Volf needs perspective."

"You didn't see him almost lose his breakfast down in the catacombs."

She shrugged and tried not to look at him too long. Tried not to let him see her crumbling. The colder she became, the more his gaze burned.

"How did you manage to get everyone to leave a funeral unfinished on Allhallowsmas?"

He grinned shamelessly. "Oh, I just asked very nicely. Works wonders."

Friede found her face thawing slowly. Not quite into a smile, but dangerously close.

"Now I imagine we have about until noon before the whole town knows and Volf goes into cardiac arrest," he added.

"Maybe that will teach him some sympathy for the dead."

"*Fee.*"

The nickname shocked her like a caress.

Friede found the mettle to look him in the face. It was like looking into the sun glinting off snow. "*Bast*," she mimicked.

"Are you all right?" he asked, and her petulance evaporated as quickly as it'd come.

She could tell him the truth. About how she wanted to go. She should tell him. This could be the last day they ever spent side by side, and he was the best friend she'd ever had. Even during the days when he drank too much, the stretches of the silent treatment after every argument, whether fair or unfounded, she couldn't remember a time she hadn't loved him. He would understand. She knew he would.

"No," she admitted. But the rest wouldn't come out.

Bast had never balked at her sad, bitter truths before, but she feared this might be the one to break everything.

More than he'd already broken things, added that small, icy voice inside her, bitterer still.

Even if they found Death's skull, brought Eluned back, put everything to rights, Friede knew there would be no perfect moment; those words would shatter everything. She couldn't hurt him like that.

He turned to her, curls glistening with hailstones like a crown of tiny pearls. "What can I do?"

Friede turned to face the wind. The weather was dithering again, and the sudden spray of rain soaked her hair and shoulders. She started carefully down the cobblestone steps toward town. Bast fell in step close behind. Damn her cowardice, but she couldn't bring the words to her cold lips.

She focused on keeping her gait measured and even, then her voice. "Let's start by finding that kid who took the skull and I'll think about it."

"Maybe took the skull," Bast corrected.

"Maybe," she echoed. For some reason, the word went down sour, like a lie.

CHAPTER THREE

DEAD ENDS

"Across the river," Bastian directed, slipping an arm through Friede's as the road silvered over with frost. "Mausoleum Row."

The hail and icy rain had mostly petered out by the time they grew near enough to spot the two parallel blocks of brick apartments jutting from the horizon. Their edifices crawled with creeper vines, green bandages for old bullet holes. They'd been hospitals first and still bore the faded paint identifying them as such, then converted to charity housing after the Angel of Death blotted Cairney from modern maps and memory. The buildings' weathered eaves slopped out a steady stream of melt.

Bast directed her to a door, stamping slush from his feet at the threshold. Inside was dry and sparse but well-kept. Friede headed, sighing, for the stairwell. It was cramped as a coffin, forcing them single-file in the dimness.

"You've come out here before?" she asked, shimmying around a tight corner.

"For Kamil, yeah." Bast's shoulders brushed the walls on either side and brought up a sheen of plaster dust. "A few times. They have a couple of other haunts, but this is the one they consider home. Where they lived before their parents skipped town."

Friede paused, unsure she'd heard correctly. "Skipped town? Without their child?"

"Kamil is adamant it was a planned vacation to visit relatives down south," he replied with a frown, "but it's been too long. They stayed here alone for three weeks before I could convince them that a bed at the church might be a more practical option. Volf took us both in around the same time, actually."

Friede rested for a moment on the landing. "And are they — coming back?"

Bast's lips screwed up into a line that begged her not to make him say it, the ugly thing they both knew.

Kamil's parents might have made it out of town. Maybe they had intended to come back. But more likely, they were dead under a snowdrift less than a mile beyond the pale.

Cairney's inherent remoteness hadn't protected them from the war, but now the forest that fenced them in had a funny way about it. A possessiveness in the hallowed ground that repelled visitors as well as egress. The only outsider to ever pick their way through the Pallwood in Friede's memory was Lor. She'd come as a refugee, but the ground recognized her as a descendant from a Cairney family that had moved away some generations before the bloodshed, returning alone when a newer conflict devoured the westward cities, and her family with it. Friede had been surprised when they first met by how much Lor reminded her of the older corpses in Cairney; she moved and spoke like someone on borrowed time. An outsider who felt like an old friend.

Friede's legs shuddered and threatened to give out mid-step at the crest of the fourth floor, their destination. She thrust a hand against the wall for balance. Old paint crackled away under her palm. She told herself it was the winding stairs, and not the distorted memory of Lor that billowed to the surface, making her dizzy, but even then, she didn't believe it. That last glimpse of her wife's face from underwater haunted her still. Those wide, wild eyes. Those beautiful hands. She wondered if she would ever be free of their weight.

Don't be afraid. In love there is no end.

The words erupted from her psyche unbidden, a sudden jolt at the same moment Bast's hand encircled her shoulder. She gasped, flinching too hard, she stumbled into the adjoining hall.

Those were the last words Lor had spoken to her before holding her under the lake. She knew it instinctively, immediately, and just as quickly thrust the thought away like she had her wedding ring. She needed to be steady now. There was work to do.

"Sorry, sorry." Bastian stopped himself halfway from reaching for her.

Foolishly, Friede wanted to cling to him. The urge took a remarkably long time to pass. But when he came to her side again, she had remembered herself and forced her legs out. One in front of the other in front of the other.

Bast indicated a door with a nod, and she knocked lightly on it. It lurched open.

"Kamil Kant?" she said into the gloom.

After no response, Bast piped up, "It's Bastian Ruz, from the church."

Still nothing. Friede nudged the door the rest of the way open and stepped in.

The living area was only slightly larger than Volf's office. A tall window pocked with glistening droplets lit the space, while wax from candles long gone cold puddled across the sill. Sparse furniture on the floor and walls; Friede wondered if it had always been this way, or if Kamil's parents had only plucked their favorites to take with them out of town. It left just enough negative space that she couldn't decide which was the likelier story. Though if she were Kamil Kant, she imagined it had enough marrow left to nourish a feeble hope for the latter.

Almost all the doorposts in the apartment held small charms, scrolls wrapped in delicate ceramic cases that Friede recognized from one of the older faiths in Cairney, protections Kamil's family had opted to leave for them. In one of the bedrooms, the linens had been stripped, and a handful of empty hangers dangled in the closet. In the other, a petite bed and a piano that took up the entirety of one wall. It was a lovely studio model, the same one that Friede had personally seen replaced with the upright in the school's music room. She had known the old piano had been spirited away to a family in town, but never which one.

She ran her fingers over the keys, smiling to find them free of dust. A smatter of sheets lay on the desk.

"I only assign sonatas like these to advanced classes. How old is Kamil?"

"Just turned fifteen," Bast said, coming up behind her.

Friede's brows rose.

"I knew you'd like them," he added with a smirk.

The bed adjacent was mussed, crocheted blankets thrown half to the floor, a trail Friede's eye followed to a section of floorboard that sat slightly crooked from its brethren. She crouched to peer underneath, leaning on the frame to ease the tremor in her calves, and gingerly wiggled her fingers into the gap.

Inside the crevice sat a box, small enough to almost fit in her palm. She drew it out.

The box was decked in an old floral fabric that clung to yellowing glue. She held it up to Bast for examination, prodding open the rusted clasp.

A few small baubles jostled around within: a switchblade with a pearlescent handle, a tarnished iron nail, a collection of smooth river stones, and a jagged piece of clear crystal.

Friede jolted. "They've been in my house," she marveled, drawing out the crystal. It caught the muted light and sent shimmering flashes across the wall. "From the chandelier in the entryway."

Friede hadn't actually stepped foot in that house since her

murder, though it still belonged to her on paper. Bast had gathered the necessities left behind for her and helped her settle into a cozy one-bedroom by the garden district as soon as she'd been able to walk again. The house she grew up in was all alone now, wasting away there by the edge of the lake. She tried to picture a young child roaming the halls, plucking memories from the detritus. At least it was useful to someone still.

Hand shaking, Friede shut the crystal back in the box and slipped it snugly into the pocket of her coat. The click it made was too loud in the little room.

"What are you doing?"

Friede couldn't convince her legs to lift her back up. "It'll encourage Kamil to talk with us if we have something they want."

Bast's mouth puckered the way it did when he wanted to argue. "Fee ..."

He always could tell when she was keeping something from him. From the moment they'd met, he had a second sense for her moods, if not her motivations. Friede could never decide whether or not to be touched or annoyed by his careful attention.

Though he obviously had something in mind already, she was hesitant to give him the satisfaction of thinking he could read her so easily. She couldn't say where such an adolescent urge had come from.

"What?" she said, petulant.

His voice was overly gentle, infuriatingly so. "I know this must be hard. Are you sure you need to be doing this?"

Leaning heavily on the bed frame, she stood. There was a cold snap in her voice as she answered, "You haven't said her name once, you know. Both you and Volf, just carrying on like normal, while Eluned is ..." Her throat gave a pang. "Eluned is dead, and no one seems to care but me. She didn't strangle herself, Bast. It happened in the church — it's probably someone we know. That doesn't bother you?"

He stepped closer. His expression unfurled with sympathy, no judgment even in its edges. "Of course it does. I just ... don't want you to dwell on it like this. It's not your burden to bear just because you found her." His eyes flicked to her neck and back up. "I'm sorry you had to see her like that."

A bitter laugh perched on the back of Friede's tongue. She kept it down. It was easier this way, to slip into grief for Eluned instead of herself. She welcomed the distraction.

This hurt wasn't a burden. It was the sharpest feeling she had left, and Friede would be damned before she let it go.

"I just mean ... we can do this together. It's not all on you."

Friede kept her shoulders straight, her face blank. "I thought we were."

Bast didn't reply, just reached for her hand and squeezed it, eyes on the floor.

Even if he didn't know it, he was offering to help her secure the means of leaving him forever. His touch made Friede want to weep, or scream, or break something. Anything but tell him the truth. The thought of venturing into the rest of this day alone terrified her more than she could say. She couldn't risk losing him, not with so little time left.

The fear won out like it always did. All she could do was nod, hoping he sensed her gratitude, and entwined their fingers.

Out in the main room, the old floor creaked.

Friede's head snapped to the sound. She pulled away from Bast involuntarily.

There was something to the cadence of the steps that set her teeth on edge, scraping against dead nerves on the back of her neck. Too heavy to belong to a child like Kamil. The sound had her trembling like a teen caught out past curfew again, alight with fear and desperate for familiar shadows.

Bast had always evaded his parents' detection easily on those nights, while Friede's own were happy enough that she had a friend to sneak out with in the evenings; they'd rarely ever run into trouble.

But the instincts of those youthful indiscretions seemed to have fled Bast entirely now, as he made to turn toward the sound, or even worse, to speak. Acting without thought, Friede grasped him by the collar and pulled him sharply back, cutting off sound. Her mind raced. Just beside the bed was a small closet; as quietly as she could, she ushered them both through the door and slid it carefully shut, leaving only the smallest crack to peer through.

She had to bend her knees awkwardly to fit in the space, and the width was scarcely better, forcing her flush to Bast. Friede craned her head to one side to keep his hair out of her eyes. He went perfectly still, arms braced at stiff angles, though she felt his smile's curve brush her clavicle. Friede was suddenly grateful she no longer had to breathe or blush.

She waited, watching for the intruder to reveal themselves. Those steady, hushed footfalls continued in the other room, their lilting, irregular rhythm sending a slow shiver up Friede's spine. She tensed as they drew closer, and closer still, until she could have sworn they entered the bedroom. But she saw no one. Not even a shadow, a stirring of dust.

Bast must have noticed it too. He muttered, "What the hell?"

The footsteps came again, moving away, their previous calm abandoned.

Friede thrust open the closet door and clattered out, Bast clipping her ankle as she took off in an unbalanced jog, dropping her cane and following the footfalls out of the apartment and into the hall.

"Who's there?" she demanded of the air, trying to sound authoritative though her voice and legs shook.

She couldn't tell if the beat of the boards thrumming was her own tread, or Bast's, or the other intruder's. The hallway was empty either way, no sign of anyone living or dead, just an echo that unspooled in every direction at once.

Friede cursed as Bast caught up behind her. She gave an incredulous shrug. "I don't understand."

Bast offered her cane; she took it stiffly, their eyes meeting and abruptly separating.

"I'll check the other end," he said.

Friede watched him shuffle down the far side of the hall for a moment before turning to the stairwell. She still felt the impression of his weight around her, like she would find his smile among the bouquet of bruises at her throat.

She shook her head and descended to the landing. It was only a few more steps, but one leg buckled without warning, and she stumbled against the wall, striking her elbow at an angle that made the muscles twitch violently. Her cane slipped from her fingers. It rolled, but stopped suddenly before it could pitch the rest of the way down the stairs.

Friede stared, and stared, unable to make a sound as the air before her ever so slightly rippled.

When the ripple touched her, it was almost gentle, like a breeze. Just enough to tousle a few hairs and brush the crest of her cheek.

What—

The word never left her throat, never reached the air, because all at once there was no room left in Friede for words or thought or sound. She was wrested sharply out of her body and cast into a whiteout gale. Stuck watching from somewhere both close and far, bigger than the sky and small as a flake of snow on the wind.

In a blink, a thousand images skittered over her eyes, bleeding in and out of each other.

Footsteps crunching in solid snow, along the edge of the river where she and Lor walked and whispered long into the night. Tiny flakes melting on stone. Snow falling beyond the windows while they huddled at the piano in the church, hand over hand on the keys, keys like white snow.

Sometimes she tasted blood on Lor's kisses; her lungs were never the same after the shelling. Sometimes she woke in the night, wheezing red into her hand. Sometimes she flushed so dark Friede worried she'd burst like a berry. Red lips screaming. Eluned's gaping wound-mouth. A fist with knuckles split and bloody. Blood dripping from Lor's mouth into her eyes as she weakened and bruised under the weight of her wife, the weight of water dragging her under.

The old willow bowing to the lake. The pale-barked trees she and Bast ran through as children, climbed gnarled branches to touch the sky, hid beneath in perfect silence when the world turned cruel. Bast saying her arms were like the branches, skinny and white, but he felt safe there too.

The images all careened. Turned to nonsense.

Bloody snow. Snowy trees. Blood on teeth. Blood on the leaves.

With every flicker, the wind between and behind it all. Wind on her face, in her mouth, between her ribs, so sharp and so cold.

There, on the wind, she saw something. Felt it.

Something stirring.

Stirring into a shape, like a puff of chimney smoke, and just as light. It grew with each puff. When the breeze couldn't hold it anymore, it started to crawl.

Little finger marks in the crusted snow. Little furrows and sighs. Little lidless eyes gouging dark strokes into the slushy roadside.

A head full of blood and cold and something harder and heavier. A cancer choking thought, and breath, and hope. Growing with each furrow in the frozen ground. Inch by agonized inch.

One, then another, and another, on and on and on until ...

A name.

A name slipped from the shape's paper-thin tongue. She felt the ache of it, how just the effort of speaking tore a bloodless wound into its jagged mouth, a cry no one heard.

No one.

No one but Friede.

Friede.

"Friede!"

She heard glass shatter, felt pressure break against her skull, her skull that was ringing, ringing, as Bastian appeared above her. Far above, lurching over the top of the stairs. His steps were like gunshots, each one sending lightning up her spine. But it was no longer that gale, the rippling that'd had her like a shard in its teeth.

The ceiling of the stairway stretched above her, its grain a dizzying but welcome sight. Friede felt like she'd been wrung and twisted at every joint. She'd fallen somehow, caught by the landing of the third floor. That was all. A momentary blackout, her dead gray matter struggling for stimuli and conjuring up its own.

A very small, very bad dream. But it was over now.

It was over, but the world still spun, her thoughts cast about like snowflakes when Bast's arms came around her shoulders and lifted gently. His cursing hooked her back to the moment. Friede drew her tongue across her teeth, testing that she still had them all. She thought so.

She thought ...

She didn't quite trust her thoughts at the moment. They ran distorted, streams of melt down a windowpane.

A point of clarity: Kamil Kant's box of treasures pressing a dent in her side, seemingly unharmed. Small mercies.

"What happened? Did you fall?"

That much was obvious. The rest she wasn't so sure of.

"Yes," she replied. Then, "Who was that?"

Bast shrugged. "Fuck if I know. A ghost?"

A knot came loose behind Friede's ribs, and she laughed, sputtering a little. "That's blasphemy."

He sounded like his father; the most irreverent man Friede had ever met. She had to remind herself, even as she hiccupped faintly, that his family had never been religious in the Cairney fashion; her resurrection had sent him over to the other side, toward devotion. To hear him now, a cleric of Death, contradicting the basic dogma of the clerisy so casually, she could barely contain herself. A flash of the old Bastian peeking from the fresh paint of the new.

Eventually, he started to look down at her with some worry, so

Friede tucked her head under his pillowy chin and clasped him back. She had to savor moments like these while she still could. There wouldn't be many left, if she had her way.

Don't let go, she thought, the only solid thing left rattling around her skull.

"Okay, fuck this," Bast said. "I need a drink."

CHAPTER FOUR

CUT CLEAN

The trek from Mausoleum Row back toward the river seemed to take hours.

Sometimes Friede felt her frigid death more acutely, how Lor and the rimy water had sapped the strength from her limbs, leaving them little sturdier than twigs wrapped in ice. She leaned heavily against Bastian as they went. The sight of the bright snow after that awful stupor on the stairs shocked her. The streaks of mud churned up by coach wheels and boots resembled deep wounds; all of it reminded Friede of those invisible fingers knuckling their way in, dragging something incomprehensible behind them.

She didn't want to see it. Still, she circled back again and again to the thought. Those thoughts she didn't trust. The footsteps with no maker. That strangled ripple in the air and breeze before she came untethered.

It was a little like its own death, Friede thought.

Or a resurrection.

It was nothing, she corrected. But even her inner voice shook.

Friede knew there were no such things as ghosts. At least not here. They were a superstitious relic of a buried age, one that died with the old Cairney. Either souls had a home or they didn't. If they weren't resurrected, they lingered in that dark desolation until the next unstitching of the veil sucked them into the next world, either shepherded by Death to eternal rest, or, untended, to oblivion. It simply wasn't possible for there to be a ghost in Cairney.

And yet.

And yet that knowledge wasn't the slightest bit comforting after what she'd seen. What she'd felt. It chewed at her like rot.

She clasped tighter to Bast. He returned the gesture, patting her hand lightly. He showed no exertion for having shouldered a significant part of her weight for the entire journey. She knew of the hidden strength in his soft frame, strength enough to have carried her waterlogged corpse across half of Cairney to be resurrected in the catacombs. Maybe, doing so had made him strong. That night had made them both a lot of things.

Her arm snug with his as they walked, Friede got to thinking again of goodbyes.

Would it be better, kinder, to get it over with quickly? A clean cut to spare them both some mess.

Friede made herself a hesitant bargain: a rest, first. To clear her head, steady her hand. Then she would make the cut.

The best pub in Cairney leaned precariously on the edge of the river, close enough that the north-facing wall sparkled with a thin mist and had grown fuzzy with moss. A Stiff Drink was the first building to see when crossing the bridge, and the last stop before leaving. Always busy, but patrons never seemed to loiter in want of a table. The bell above the door gave a tinny chime as they bumbled in.

"Don't think I don't know you're still cut off," Friede said, doing her best to speak over the chatter.

Bast's laugh rose easily above the din, a bright clap. "Damn, I was hoping you'd forgotten." He flashed her a wink. "Yes, thanks for the reminder. But you're not."

Neither of them could get any benefit from the booze anymore, which he knew, but Friede let the jest pass without further remark.

The air was stale and smoky inside the bar. Friede had always found it ironic that the owner and proprietor of the pub was a living man: Clay Toussaint, who paced smoothly by the taps and waved at their arrival, his beard long and braided and his head hairless. Friede taught his two daughters piano, and subsequently hadn't paid for her own drinks in years.

Much of Cairney turned to running similarly on favors and good turns instead of coin after Death swept in — more so among the devout families rather than those like Bast's, who didn't attend funerals or other church gatherings regularly. She recalled more than one schoolyard brawl incited by the other children calling Bast and his parents damned for their worldliness. Their first official meeting had taken place when Friede, irate at the mocking, attempted to intervene in one such altercation. She and Bast had made their introductions over matching bloody noses that day. The teasing hadn't stopped, but once they were a pair, it stung far less than before.

Of course, the dead didn't require things like drink, or music, or fine clothes, or rouge for their cheeks. Death had freed them of decay as well as digestion. But that never steered anyone away. Those that imbibed would retch everything out back with the refuse, then return for another round. It was all for appearances. Habit. They needed it. To feel alive.

Friede gracelessly straddled a stool at the bar and offered a polite smile as Toussaint drifted over. She folded her hands in her lap and tried to keep the tremors from settling back in. "Good morning, Clay."

"Afternoon now," he rumbled. He gave Bast only a short nod. "Get you anything?" He spoke directly to her, his gaze somewhat questioning. It was uncommon for her to be here aside from lesson days. The last time she'd sat at this bar was with Lor, who'd had an amusing sweet tooth when it came to wine.

By his own request, no pub in Cairney served Bastian Ruz anything but water anymore, but his hands still grew restless when they stood in sight of any liquor. Like dying drunk meant he could never be completely free of the craving.

She shouldn't have agreed to come here with him. The blunder was obvious now, but she'd been too distracted earlier to make another suggestion. The bar was his favorite.

She shook her head at Clay, but kept her eyes on Bast as he leaned one arm on the bar and stood facing her, fidgeting more than usual with the bone set into his ring.

Clay nudged two glasses of water their way, likely by force of habit, and wandered off. Friede thought his gaze might have lingered on her for a moment. She tugged the edges of her collar up higher.

"This was a bad idea, wasn't it?" she muttered.

He smirked. "It's bad, but not your worst."

"What was my worst?" Not coming to his funeral, if she had to make a guess. They hadn't spoken of it. But then, he hadn't come to her wedding. Even in cowardice, they were a perfect match.

He made a show of studying her from top to bottom, but she thought he deliberately avoided meeting her eyes. "Those shoes with that shirt."

She kicked him in the shin, and he laughed loud enough to draw stares.

As if to collect himself, Bast downed his water in several strained gulps that he would surely regret in not too long. He kept his fingers tight on the empty glass.

There was nothing close to silence here, but the vortex of quiet that expanded between them turned Friede's stomach to knots.

Did he know she was lying to him? Did he despise her already?

Friede felt she was still seeing the world from upside-down on those stairs, struggling for balance. Her gut braced for freefall.

"You still haven't told me if we're on for the dance, you know," he said suddenly.

The words took a few moments to settle. "What?"

"The dance," he said, slower this time. After a beat of staring mournfully at the bottom of his glass, he glanced up. "You're not going to stand me up, are you?"

Her throat tightened. A phantom ache started up behind her eyes. She couldn't bear to think of Allhallowsmas and celebration right now. The dance at the end of the night was their one tradition, kept since adolescence. He still made a point of asking her permission every year.

The first time he'd asked her, they were thirteen and fourteen, and she'd laughed at the idea. It was the same the year after that. The year after that, she'd said yes, and they'd thought it a great jest to wear each other's school uniforms instead of the formal attire required. She'd lost count of the number of times Bast had tripped on the too-long legs of her trousers that night.

He kept up the game even after their school days had concluded, once appearing on her doorstep in a dress, offering a suit he'd picked out just for her. Her favorite year was when they'd been caught in a storm on the way to the church, and both had the worst colds of their lives the morning after.

He committed to the tradition even when his drinking had started to drown him. She'd wanted to say no that time, but couldn't bear to see him sullen, and took him home when he'd vomited all over both of their finery.

The dance after that, six years ago now, had no dancing for either of them. Just Bast holding her sobbing in his arms on the church steps after she'd bid farewell to her parents. Then, in the inverse of a prior year, he'd taken her home and bundled them both into bed under every quilt he could find, promising to get her warm again.

Friede studied him and understood he was offering her an out. An opportunity to unburden herself. He'd seen right through her like always.

Would it be cruel, she wondered, or a last kindness to grant him that before she left?

It wasn't the clean cut she'd promised herself. But maybe she didn't want things to end cleanly after all.

Maybe she wanted to leave a scar. Like he had when he chose to resurrect her.

Friede reached for her water, fingertips tracing the notes of a requiem in the condensation. Her tongue was near lead as she answered, "Ask me again once we've found the skull."

He smirked, but it didn't reach his eyes. "Such a one-track mind."

She took a gulp of water to steady herself and immediately regretted it. The cold slithered down achingly slow.

"We could try the house next." She tested each word like a step on an old floorboard. Feeling for cracks. "If Kamil has been there before, they could be hiding out there now."

Bast made a noncommittal sound, but didn't reply.

"It's still mine on paper." With great effort, she added, "Lor didn't take the keys."

"Friede, enough," he interjected, exasperated. The sudden iciness in his tone shocked her; Friede's knuckles knocked into her glass, sloshing cold water onto her sleeve.

Bast leaned in. "You don't have to do this. Any of it. You don't owe Eluned or Volf anything." After a moment, he added, "or me."

She wanted to laugh at his ignorance. Of course she owed Eluned.

Eluned had been the only one not to rebuff her grieving after her death. To listen, to accept her questions, not to offer useless platitudes. To truly see her.

Bast wanted to coddle her. Like he thought she couldn't handle death.

She wasn't a cleric, but she dealt with corpses almost as often. She was more than capable of seeing this through. She wasn't doing this for Volf or him, not even solely for Eluned. She was doing this for her. Because no one deserved to die like that. And for some reason, Friede seemed to be the only person in Cairney not afraid to admit that. Resurrection made no difference. Murder was murder. Lor had gotten away with it. Friede wouldn't let them sweep another stolen life under the rug.

"Bastian Ruz, are you trying to get rid of me?"

He reached for her hand like he had in the tenement.

"I just don't want to see you hurt," he replied, quick and quiet, like a confession.

Friede pulled away. Her hand knocked into her glass, tipping it over. The spill cascaded down the bartop. Cold streams encircled her wrist. Something brittle inside her buckled; she stood from her stool. Caught in the teeth of that terrible chill, she grasped for the first warmth that came to hand. It was anger, bubbling just under the surface of her hurt.

"It's too late for that, and you know it."

Bast visibly winced. It sent a sympathetic pang through her, but she bit down on her cheek until it passed. She had to say the words before they burned through her. No more coddling.

"Did you already forget how you decided that I would live after I died? What more do you want? Am I not capable of making my own choices?"

"I ... I never said you weren't," he said, half rising.

He could have said he was sorry. Instead, he just looked up at her with those wide, supplicating eyes. The same look he'd cast her when she woke in the catacombs in his arms, cold and empty.

She couldn't give him what he wanted. There was no going back for either of them.

"You never asked. Not once did you ask what I wanted. You just did as you liked," Friede said. "And now... and now you want to tell me over and over again what I do and don't have to do, what I do or don't owe, like it'll somehow absolve you." She ached to take a breath, to have tears pour out and take the mess inside her with them. It made the words sting all the more. "Here's what I'd like to do. I'd like to go to my house and find the skull, and once I have it, I'd like to leave Cairney. Tonight. For good. You can't decide for me this time."

Bast reached again and caught her wrist. A slow trickle of realization darkened his face. His usual easy expression faded, revealing lines and a frown Friede didn't recognize. He seemed an entirely different man suddenly. A beautiful stranger.

"Friede ..." he murmured, but didn't finish the plea.

She slipped free of his grip and found her cane with shaking hands. "Don't you dare follow me," she said, and turned away, letting the waves of the crowd swallow her.

CHAPTER FIVE

STIFFED

Friede's knuckles rapped hard and untimely against the washroom sink; she couldn't manage to settle on a rhythm. Her thoughts kept interrupting in fits and starts. She muttered lip-curled curses to the cracked porcelain and avoided meeting her reflection's eye in the mirror.

So much for a clean cut. So much for relief. Friede didn't know why she'd expected anything else.

No more secrets now, at least. She'd told Bast the truth, and he could hate her if he wanted. That craving was satisfied, but she didn't feel the least bit better. Only ugly, bloodstained.

A glance to the door brought up panic like bile. She didn't think she could face him again after this. She might forgive him if he looked at her with those wide, pleading eyes again. She was fragile as a snowflake, close to melting at all times.

And what did she have to show for it?

Friede massaged her brow, fingers contending hopelessly with rigid skin. She had half a mind to crawl out the window situated near the ceiling of the washroom and be done with this mortifying business altogether. She was clever, if not quick.

Maybe she could solve this on her own. That would show Bast; she didn't need to be coddled or protected from hurt. She knew this kind of death better than he did. Better than any of the clerics could hope to.

It was a tempting thought, running. And it would make her even more of a coward. Did she really want to spend her last hours running from her oldest friend, the only true friend she had left in all of Cairney?

But the alternative turned her stomach just as much.

Just as she was studying the window, trying to calculate if her shoulders would even fit through its thin mouth, a pair of snowy boots appeared beyond the glass, kicking up wakes of mud-black slush. They skidded past, then came back around and paused. A pair of hands came next, then a screech as the hinge was forced open and the figure began shoving themselves bodily in. Friede stumbled back just in time to avoid those dripping boots connecting with her head.

She watched in stupefied fascination as the boots gave way to torn wool stockings, then finally, a child in a boxy coat, with thick dark hair cropped to their chin and deep umber skin to match. They dropped to the floor with a short, shuddering breath. The window clammed shut, the sound making them both jolt. The snow caked on their shoes and shoulders began to melt almost immediately, casting off a trail of dark droplets as they turned and brushed themselves off, only to find Friede directly in their path.

"Shit," they muttered, then flinched in the fashion of someone oft-corrected, steps faltering. "Uh, sorry."

Their cheeks were round and flushed from the cold. Friede guessed they couldn't have been more than sixteen.

She stuttered through several replies that didn't manage to form full words, in which time the child had winged around her and began trying the door. The fingers that darted out of their coat sleeves were startlingly lean. Friede stared for a long moment, struck still and reeling at the fog their gusting breath made on her skin. That coat on their back almost certainly had belonged to Bastian about ten years ago. That fact, coupled with those narrow fingers strangling the doorknob, had Friede's mouth gaping wide.

"Kamil Kant?" she blurted.

Their hands fumbled on the lock. A tendon in their neck twitched, but they didn't fully turn. Friede had the feeling if she didn't act now, the child would vanish on the next breeze and never be caught again.

"Please don't go," she said. "I'm — my name is Friede Inkerman. I need to talk to you."

They raised a thick brow and finally looked Friede in the eye for longer than half a second. Their shoulders were drawn up with bowstring tension.

One hand still lingering on the door, the other tight against their side, they said in a low voice, "I know who you are."

Friede had first thought it was simply exertion winding up their wiry frame, but from this new angle, their unease was clear in a deep-furrowed brow and the raw, chewed bloody state of their lip. A hunted rabbit kind of fear.

Friede didn't know what to do with that realization. She reached into her coat and drew out the box, hoping the sight of it would keep them moored in place for a few moments more. "You are Kamil Kant, aren't you? This is yours?"

Their eyes flicked from Friede to the box, back to Friede. She didn't expect the way their posture tightened: wrists flexing, fingers curled into a fist, ready to strike out.

"How — Who the fuck do you think you are?" Finally, they faced her, the whites of their eyes shot through with red, but still the brunt of their searing stare had Friede balking, even half-lidded through dark eyelashes.

"I'm a pianist—"

"I said I know that!"

Friede was thrown, suddenly, her feet planted on a receding shore. That happened, sometimes, with a brain as waterlogged as hers. Things slipped through the cracks. She hated how it shook her, not knowing her own beginnings and endings. "I … Ha — have we met?"

The ferocity in their eyes dampened some, cooled by her confusion.

"No," they replied. "But I've been to funerals. And Seleny talks about you some."

She grasped after the thread of familiarity. "Seleny Toussaint?"

No reply, just a frown drawn into a thin, stubborn line. Friede fought to think back. None of her students had ever mentioned Kamil by name, she thought. But …

"That's right," she said, a memory breaching. "Seleny said she'd been practicing more with someone … someone special." The second part had only been implied, but Friede knew her intuition was correct from the way Kamil's cheeks darkened with a fresh flush.

"So what? What do you want? Why did you take my things?" They drifted closer now, but the air of threat had winnowed to only mild distrust, curiosity a thrumming undercurrent.

Friede wanted nothing more than to take a deep breath and let the truth spill out. She felt too full of it, a rotten fruit dangling heavy on the vine. "I needed to talk to you."

Kamil breathed out slowly. "So, talk."

The invitation sank in like a fishhook, splitting her open.

"There was a funeral this morning," she started. She took a small step forward; she didn't want to add to the child's fright, but there was no blanching the horror from the truth, no keeping the words locked any longer. "A woman was murdered during it. Or last night. I'm not entirely sure, but she was a good woman, the Anchoret, and someone — someone wrapped their hands around her throat and choked her until she died. While she was still in her bed. While she was scared and alone. No one even heard her scream."

Do you know how awful that is? she ached to ask. *I hope you never do.*

Kamil's arms dropped. They looked down and away, teeth sinking into their chapped lip, but it didn't hide the way they started to quake harder. They looked like they wanted to run. And like they'd been running all day, on the edge of exhaustion.

Sympathy burned in Friede. "You know already, don't you?"

"People die every day," they said, lip quivering. The words had the tone of something repeated but not believed. A lie used to cover a wound that hadn't stopped bleeding yet. "Anyway, don't all you church people call every death a blessing?"

Close, but not quite. She couldn't blame Kamil for the assumption.

Friede stole another step forward, acutely aware of her stiff legs, blue face, not one drop of warmth in her veins. "I don't feel blessed to be this way."

Kamil opened their mouth, deep red running down the raw valleys of her lips. Their mask of indifference had cracked and fallen away. Only a frightened child remained. Hand trembling, they reached into the recesses of their coat and pulled out a familiar white, silken shroud. Friede gasped when she saw it, but kept herself still.

"I didn't hurt her," Kamil said, breath thin, throat bobbing. "Please, believe me." The desperation in their voice was raw, almost rote, like they were used to making such a plea and having it ignored.

In the following silence, Friede swayed forward and caught the tail of the shroud. She nodded, hope sparking against her ribs. "I do, I do. But where's the skull?"

They shook their head. No, it was all of them that shook. "I can't ... The clerics will kick me out if they hear."

"Fuck the clerics," she said. "This isn't about them. I won't let them throw you out, I swear."

What did she have to swear on? Her life? Her immortal soul? Nothing much of note. Still, a part of her knew she'd get a smile out of Bastian for sheer brazenness, which was a small comfort, stoking her confidence. And on Kamil's face, too, a hint of a shocked smile at the corners of their mouth, twitching up like green shoots in spring.

The child's dark, smoldering eyes met her gaze and held it. Fire against ice. "She wasn't alone."

"What?"

"The Anchoret. I was there. She didn't die alone."

Friede's throat clenched. "Please," she pleaded. "Tell me what happened. I promise you're not in any trouble."

Kamil's gaze dropped. "I ... I can't." They stepped back and reached for the door again, chilled fingers fumbling. They left the shroud flapping from Friede's fist, caressing her cheeks like that rippling breeze from the stairwell. The room shrank down like ice in a glass. Kamil breathed hard as they retreated.

"Was it a ... a ghost?" Friede flung all of her desperation into the question, foolish as it sounded.

The child paused with their hand on the latch. Friede heard their gasp as if pricked, a shiver passing through them and jumping right into her.

They both stood silent and frozen for a moment. Friede sensed the heaviness of the truth as it pendulumed back and forth between the two of them, and she wondered which would find the heart to take hold of it first.

Kamil prevailed. They seemed to not have any strength left for denial now, but Friede still thought it a kind of courage that unlocked their lips. "We ... we call it dybbuk in my family. A spirit without a body."

Friede nodded. "I've seen it too. We crossed paths not an hour ago, at your apartment. What does it want?"

Their eyes misted. They chewed at their lip. "They're dead. They don't want to be anymore. That's why I was supposed to get them the skull."

Friede kept silent, not trusting her tongue.

Breath hitching, Kamil continued, "I only wanted to help. I didn't know. I didn't think they'd hurt anyone. She — the Anchoret — was asleep when I snuck in. I went through the window. But she woke up when I was leaving, and the ... the dybbuk ... it must have followed me, and I think it was trying to help me get away, but I didn't ... I don't know. It hurt her. It happened so fast. When it touched me, my head went all funny, I think I was out for a minute, and when I came to, the skull was gone and so was the dybbuk, and Eluned was dead. So, I ran." The confession tumbled out on one long wavering breath. They shook their head, frantic. "I just wanted to help."

Friede rested a hand on their shoulder, though it did nothing to soothe their shaking. What comfort could a dead woman offer?

"I understand," she said, though she didn't really. How could she? She could only imagine how lonely a child had to be to consort with ghosts. "This is important. Do you know where the spirit is now? What they intend to do with the skull?"

Kamil wiped at their red eyes. They sniffled, shrugging. "I only know the stories, but I'd guess they're still looking for a body. Maybe a cleric would know?" They took a deep, shaky breath, glancing at the door, then the window, then finally settling on Friede.

It should have been impossible for a spirit to wander aimlessly as they described. But today was not like other days. With the skull out of the proper hands, Cairney was hallowed no more, just like old times. Who could say what that meant for the dead. Who knew what horrors might come crawling through the veil.

If Friede's heart could beat, it would have pounded at the thought. Stubbornly, spitefully, she stood as tall as she could muster and tried to fix a look of confidence on her face. She kept her curses turned inward and said, "I know a cleric."

CHAPTER SIX

THE LAKE OF TEARS

Bast's stool at the bar was empty when Friede returned to it, Kamil at her heels. A napkin sat under his drained glass, creased with ink in his nigh-unreadable hand.

'Following your lead.'

Something in her chest pulled taut, plucking at dead sinew and bone. She didn't have the strength to try unraveling it. Instead, she shoved the napkin into her pocket beside the shroud and stepped out into the cold.

They hailed a cab for the journey uptown. Though it bounced and jolted enough to disarticulate her skeleton, Friede was grateful for the reprieve from standing.

Kamil didn't speak another word, only stared darkly, so she passed the time thinking of Bast's fingers tracing the bone set into his ring, the vanishing footsteps in the tenement, that invisible brush of skin on her cheek, and the visions that followed. She hoped Bast had found more answers than she'd found questions.

She hoped to Death he didn't hate her now. It was a quiet hope, coddled close and scraping against an angry edge of hurt, but she hoped it all the same.

When the cab deposited them at her old street, the sight of the graying house knifing up at its end sent ice water through Friede's veins. Glass crunched underfoot as they climbed the steps to the porch, shattered shards from the windows her parents had crafted. Their colors were brilliant still, an entire forest's worth of greens and blues and yellows strewn like chaff.

Friede hesitated, leaning so heavily on her cane that every joint in her arm trembled. The longer she waited there, the more the greenery obscuring the arches seemed to sway, inching closer and closer, hungry for rot. She wondered how much decay had gorged on the place in her absence. At her, too.

She didn't much want to uncover the answer to that question now that it stared her in the face, but Kamil made the decision for her, striding forward and shouldering their way in.

The door guttered open with a wet gasp. A moment after stepping inside, Kamil paused, nose crinkling. Indoors was even worse for wear than Friede had expected. The few months had not been kind since her departure. Weeds had begun to worm up through the floor; damp ate at the runners and boards; curtains pooled in soggy heaps by more shattered windows. The chandelier lay like a beached leviathan in the center of the entryway, crystal shards scattered to every corner. Friede resisted the urge to reach for those that still dangled together. She craved any sound to break up the monotony of her suppurating footsteps as she surveyed the wreckage, but touching it seemed too much like desecrating the dead.

Amid the detritus, she gathered no obvious signs of Bast's presence, but couldn't bring herself to call out for him. She thought she might scream, or find stale water if she opened her mouth. The cobwebs in the corners were heartier than her.

It seemed impossible that any happiness had ever dwelt here. Without Friede, or Lor, or her parents, it'd simply fallen apart, gutted of all splendor.

From the open doorway at her back, a dull plinking as Kamil found one of her greatest regrets: the grand piano left among the ruins, sounding just as bloated and spoiled as all the rest. She continued her march to join them in the music room; they stood plucking idly, wincing at the discordant notes spat out by the keys.

"It's ruined," Kamil said. It was an accusation. "Why'd you leave it?"

Why had she? "Death and resurrection don't lend themselves to particularly rational decisions."

They scoffed, obviously disbelieving.

"I was grieving. And it hurt too much to look back on the life I'd had before," she confessed.

Kamil tried again and again to draw a melody from the keys, but the wood and strings were all rotten through. "But you're here now."

"Yes."

"And?"

Friede gently lowered the fallboard. "And it still hurts the same."

Without a response, Kamil made quick work of the boggy floor and flitted out of the room.

Friede followed, though she seemed to find every dip and snag as she limped between the halls. In the kitchen, a small tree had buckled one side of the roof, and leaves caked the floor in a carpet of brown that clung to her shoes. Every inch of the room dripped. A filmy sheen coated the table where Friede had taken her tea every morning.

Two glasses and a bottle of wine stood sentinel, wreathed in a mix of dust and frost.

Friede's last breath rioted in her chest. Only half in control of her limbs, she reached out slowly toward the glasses, remembering that last sip's sweetness, and Lor's kiss that had chased it. Both memories were sour now.

Sourer still was the bite in her chest where Lor's presence had come to reside. The love was a thorny wraith of a thing, its scar tissue snarled around the edges of the knife her wife had left behind.

She'd never expected to fall in love. The stories and songs of her adolescence had been saturated with romance, but the reality of the thing never once felt the least bit within her reach, especially where physical intimacies were concerned. Mortal flesh never held much appeal compared to her muses. She was nothing like Bast, who proudly took lovers of all genders and creeds and lit up any room he stepped into like a private sun. She was stilted and brooding and cold even before death, and most people glanced off her icy edges. Friede had told herself a thousand times that she didn't mind the solitude, and had even started believing the lie. But Lor changed things.

When she'd appeared in the endmost pew at a funeral one day and complimented Friede's piano playing, Friede had already heard the whispers about a newcomer to town, but Lor had been the only one present not to treat her like one more ritual set dressing. They'd spent the rest of that day together, touring the church, walking the riverside, sharing supper at Clay's, and when they parted, she thought of nothing but Lor. The way the warmth of her blush chased away the worst of Cairney's chill. The soft, premature grays woven through her short, dark hair. The chirping soprano of her laugh. So, they saw each other the next day, and the next after that, until Friede found she quite hated being apart from her.

Staring at those glasses, Friede missed her desperately, hauntingly. Even knowing it was Lor's hands bruised forever into her throat. It was a briery kind of love, but love all the same.

Don't be afraid. In love there is no end.

Those words, again. That knife twisting.

Friede remembered waking hours after sharing that wine-tinged kiss in this kitchen, the bed empty and cold. She had known the silence of an empty house ever since her parents' deaths; it was too open, the darkness too complete. She had crept down the stairs, back to the kitchen, wrapping her shawl around her shoulders to fend off the early hour's chill. And through the frosted glass, she'd seen Lor standing there in her nightclothes, by the lake.

Mist had wafted from the water and caressed her ankles. Her edges glowed, and Friede remembered thinking what a beautiful phantom she made. As she'd crept closer, she saw her wife's lips moving.

"In love there is no end," she'd whispered. Then, "Sleeper, wake."

Lor repeated the resurrection rites once, twice, completely oblivious to Friede's reflection creeping closer in the undulating water at her feet. Friede thought Lor might have been sleepwalking as she sometimes did. But then, she started a third repetition, and the words turned strained halfway through. She choked on *sorrow,* and a wet, hacking cough tore out of her throat so violently that Friede gasped aloud despite her trepidation. Lor wheezed and retched a mist of fine red droplets into the water. That was when Friede reached for her.

When Lor turned, the last thing Friede had expected was her smile. Teeth streaked red, eyes burning with a brightness Friede had only ever seen flickers of in her during funerals, when the dead rattled back to life. She'd coughed again, and hot blood flecked onto Friede's face.

"Darling," Lor said. Her voice was strained, but the word was uttered softly, with so much fondness that Friede's throat had tightened. She drew her close, exhaling with such weight, as if punctuating a conversation Friede didn't know they'd had.

"Are you all right?" Friede had asked, laying her palm flat over Lor's heart. A calming gesture, but her pulse pounded on, a heated thrum through the fabric. She'd noticed Lor's hands trembling, but said nothing as they brushed her cheek, crawled up the rumpled collar of her nightgown.

Friede had gone still as Lor leaned in and kissed her, heedless of their bloody mouths. Softly, carefully, as if for the very first time. Then she'd said it.

"I understand now."

Friede stood still, confused.

Lor's fingers had tightened a fraction. Her eyes held the same gleam as when she'd watched her first funeral. "Don't be afraid," she whispered against Friede's lips. "In love there is no end."

She'd kissed her again, without any hint of gentleness. That was the moment Friede became afraid. But then it was too late. Lor's hands were on her throat, cutting off a scream as she dragged her from the shore; Friede had scrambled for purchase and found nothing but weeds and sucking mud. Then the cold. That inescapable cold had swallowed her up.

Now, the echo of Lor's fingers ghosted over her chin like they had before sharing that last kiss, and Friede shuddered hard. Her hip struck the table, and both glasses toppled, breaking like delicate snowflakes. Friede clung to her cane like it was the only thing keeping her from a second drowning.

When she finally managed to focus her eyes again, light from the gaping back door drew her gaze, a muffled voice wafting from the gap. Barely present in her body, Friede stumbled through.

The wind met her in a cruel embrace, all teeth. She couldn't help but freeze before the lake. The shape of that yawning blue-green mouth easily eclipsed all her dread of the house. She cast her gaze down, cowed as prey.

Just off the stone path from the back door lay a shape, halfway between her and the murmuring bank.

Even crumpled so, Friede knew the cut of Bastian's shoulders, his round cheeks, and the stripes of white hair at the top of his forehead. Kamil was there on hands and knees beside him.

Finally, Friede wrenched back her balance and hurried over. She saw a horrible flash of herself there on the shore, blue and bloated, but the image resolved, and she gasped in relief when Kamil gently turned him onto his back and his deep brown eyes caught on her, awareness glowing in their gold edges. For the span of a blink, she couldn't feel the cold anymore.

"Feeee," he slurred.

His head lolled, and one of his temples caught the light decidedly wrong.

Friede felt gingerly at the spot. Against the gentle curves of his skull, she felt a small fracture, no longer than one knuckle, but impossible to miss. Friede's unbeating heart climbed into her throat.

Injuries to the dead were a tricky business. Living flesh knew how to repair itself in good time. Dead bodies were different. Slower.

They mended like trees, if they mended at all. Remove the head from the body, and there was nothing for the soul to speak to, no nerves to puppet. With this kind of wound, only time would tell — and time felt as scarce as the breath in Friede's lungs.

"What happened?" she asked, looking around. One piece of the stepping-stone path sat askance from its siblings, its wet underside bared to the shy smudge of midmorning sun.

Bast smiled. He shifted onto one elbow; mud streaked on his sleeves. All he said was, "God, your hair's gorgeous in this light."

He reached unsteadily up to grasp at the white strands that spilled over Friede's shoulders, but couldn't quite close the distance. He sounded thoroughly drunk. Friede's hand shot out to grasp his before he could reach his goal. Then her stomach dropped, and she feared the ground might follow it.

The ring finger of his left hand was missing. A tiny shred of bone and flesh remained, bloodless and jutting at a painful angle. Bast lifted his head as if just noticing the absence.

"Your ring," Friede muttered unhelpfully.

"Oh," he groaned. "Shit." His head thunked softly back down to the muddy shore, eyes reflecting the blank sky. Friede held fast to his remaining fingers as they curled weakly around hers. He was trembling.

"What happened?" she repeated, squeezing gently but firmly to draw his attention back. "Tell me everything you remember."

He fought for words for the better part of a minute. "I ... came to say sorry ... for missing the wedding, I think. I was so late. I ... came around the back. It was snowing. The lake was freezing over. Don't know ... how I saw you like that. D'you ever think about it? How lucky that was? I just knew I had to see you ... And I did. In the water. You were dead." His chest heaved as if with sobs. Friede clutched him tighter.

"That was months ago, love." She tried to smile encouragingly through the pain. "What about today?"

He grimaced. "Right. Fuck. I came around ... the same way.

Wasn't here five minutes. And ... our invisible friend was here too. From the apartment."

"The ghost," Friede said, surprised at how quickly she accepted the new reality.

Bast chuckled in fits and starts.

"Blasphemer," he snickered, sounding just like his schoolyard bullies.

"I don't understand how it's happened, but it's the only explanation that makes a bit of sense." Friede cupped his cheek. "Did they hit you? You've got a dent here."

"They stole my fucking *finger*."

"Why ... why would they do that?" Kamil broke in. Their face had drained of color. They tried to hide the fear with a stony expression, but Friede saw past the hasty brickwork.

Bast lapsed into thought again, his eyes unfocusing for a few worrying moments. His fingers twitched against Friede's. "All the clerics have rings. It's ... soul-stuff. Picked out the bone myself."

First, the skull. Now, another relic.

Friede looked to Kamil, who chewed at their lip again. "This spirit, Kamil — you said it wanted to raise the dead?"

Kamil made a move somewhere between a shrug and a nod. Their gaze stayed fixed queasily on the gap in Bast's fingers.

Friede looked between the two of them for some kind of confirmation, encouragement, anything. But neither would meet her eye. The wind tugged her in all directions at once.

"Well, it shouldn't work," she said, more to soothe herself than anyone. "Should it?"

Bast made a noncommittal sound and looked perilously close to passing out. Which was impossible, she knew, but with the current state of affairs in Cairney, Friede wasn't about to test fate. She jerked on his arm, pulling him up into a sitting position. He went willingly, only to slump forward and rest his head on her shoulder.

His voice came out soft against her high collar: "I'm sorry, Friede. About the wedding ... and Lor. About all of this."

Friede stilled. The apology caught her off guard, a cold slap of wind. She couldn't muster a reply. Her arms went weak.

Kamil made a small, frightened sound from beside them. Friede looked to her as she braced to stand and pull Bast with her, but they'd retreated several paces back from where they'd been, hands clasping their coat tight to their frame.

"Kamil?" Her words were strangled. "What is it?"

Cold washed over her when she recognized the look they were casting into the mud. Black-eyed guilt.

They took another step back. "Lor," they said, sounding on the verge of hyperventilating. "That's them, the name the dybbuk gave me. Lor. They killed the Anchoret."

Once the words were out, Kamil inhaled sharply and took off running, as if free from a terrible weight. They skirted around the edge of the lake into the reeds, out of sight. A throng of chittering birds scattered from the observing willow to announce their passing.

It was a lucky thing Friede was already on her knees. Nothing but the hand of Death themselves could have kept her upright after hearing that name again. Kamil said it with so much fear she barely recognized it. Ice raked through her veins, the chill of the catacombs leering from her memory.

Lor.

Lor was not gone. She hadn't fled Cairney as Friede had assumed, and secretly hoped.

That had been her in the stairwell, unseen hands caressing the skin she'd bruised in death. Lor's terror, Lor's hate, bleeding through the burned-out synapses of Friede's brain.

Her name, the last word to tumble from that rotten tongue.

CHAPTER SEVEN

DEPARTED

"I don't want to die, Friede."

The first time Lor had spoken those words to her, the sun had set behind the distant birches, and Friede could barely make her out in the dark of the churchyard. Friede hadn't expected the confession; it erupted unprompted from her companion after a funeral had let out, and Lor insisted on walking her home. She'd muttered it calmly, resolute in the admission, and Friede had wanted to kiss her badly then.

She'd stepped closer until she could feel the heat of Lor's small, stoop-shouldered frame and said, "Neither do I."

Until that moment, Friede had thought Lor's curiosity for Cairney's rites only part of a wider scholar's interest in the philosophy of life and mortality. The many books Lor had collected on the subject already spilled from Friede's shelves. But it was only that night that Friede understood fully where and why the interest had taken root.

Lor had told her about the war then. How it left her trapped in rubble for two days beside the corpses of her parents and brother at only ten years old, how cities blazed so long after the bombs that the sky turned black as coal. Friede had already noted the carnage of it in the way Lor's breath rattled on every inhale, and how she stopped to cough into her sleeve often on their walks. Then the sleepwalking. She'd dreamed feverishly, and sometimes shot up screaming in the night or streaked from bed and down the halls, shaking floors and muttering about incoming raids, pounding on doors with white fists.

All the strength and pain Lor carried in her slight frame astounded Friede, but never so much as that moment she admitted her fear. Lor was the only person Friede had ever met brave enough to say those words aloud in Cairney. *I don't want to die.*

Looking back, maybe that had been the moment she'd fallen in love.

Back in the church halls, the silence hung heavy and stale like a held breath. No black-clad clerics roamed about; all their decorations for the evening's festivities lay strewn about half finished. Volf was likely still cloistered in his office, wringing his hands. The only sounds Friede noted were her shuddering footsteps on the stairs and Bast coughing apologies into her shoulder as they ascended.

"Hush, please. You're distracting me," she grunted. Though she spoke half to banish her own needling thoughts.

Lor Lor Lor, they rang.

Lor was still here. Lor had killed Eluned just like she'd killed Friede. Lor had Death's skull, and held all of their fates in her hands.

Lor was dead.

That fact cut deepest of all.

Her sweet, sickly Lor, who hadn't wanted to die. Who vowed on their wedding day to have no voyeuristic funerals, knowing just as well as Friede that lingering about as walking corpses was no blessing at all.

It seemed Death had made liars of them both.

Shame and loathing sparked a new well of energy in Friede. She crested the stairs and coaxed the door to Bast's room open with a gentle nudge of her boot, determined to finish at least one task today as she'd set out to. Dust motes danced in the air, illuminated by a stained-glass window on the far wall that painted the motley collection of donated furniture in evening-sky blue. Curled atop the unmade bed lay a fat black cat like a huge stain of soot. Its ears perked as they entered.

Bast lifted his head and grinned. "Oh, Moira." The cat mimicked his gesture, then wrinkled its pink nose at Friede.

She helped Bast the short distance past an ornate writing desk covered in various crumpled papers and lowered him to sit on the end of the bed. The cat gave a contented coo, rolling onto her back and revealing a soft gray belly. Bast almost fell onto his face reaching over to run his hand through the fur. Friede steadied him by the shoulders and used the moment of distraction to look him over again.

Instead of bruising, the skin at his temple had begun to fade from muddy olive to a light, smoke-gray. In an hour, it was likely to turn entirely white.

Friede kept one hand clenched around the shroud in her pocket. The other drifted to Bast's cheek and lingered there.

"Friede," he said abruptly, jerking up. "I want to apologize."

Her lip gave a twitch. "I think you've done more than enough of that." She tried to put a little levity into her tone, but the words came out deflated.

He shook his head. It was the first confident movement he'd made in half an hour. "Not yet. I haven't done it right yet."

"What do you mean?"

"What you said at Clay's."

Friede bristled, but didn't waver. What she had intended as a clean cut ached like a gangrenous limb, infected by the panic the last hour had piled on. Thinking on it made her feel childish.

"I was being bitter," she replied. "I shouldn't have snapped."

"No—" He grasped for her hand. "You were being honest. And I love you for it. No one else is honest with me like you."

Friede's chest gave a wretched, wanting pang. She steadied herself, planting her feet more firmly on the old boards.

"I ... I thought you were apologizing for something."

"I brought you back. When you drowned. When she ..." He

clenched his jaw. Friede thought she could hear his teeth grinding. "I'll get to her in a moment. But you ... I brought you back. Because I wanted to. When I found you, all blue and cold and so — so empty ... I was so fucking afraid. I didn't know what I'd do without you."

Her throat tightened with phantom tears. Her hand went limp in his, a floating corpse.

"I want you to have everything you want, Friede. Even if that means leaving Cairney, and me. I've been selfish. And I am so, so sorry that I've hurt you by making you stay. I'm so sorry." He pressed his forehead to the back of her hand, beseeching. It reminded her of the depictions of Death meeting with the war-torn Cairney's supplicants from Volf's books.

This was the moment for mercy. For forgiveness. The words were there, just under her tongue. They were barbed at every edge.

She could fix it all if she weren't so cold, so afraid of more pain, of change. Stitch up that ugly cut she'd made.

Bastian was the only happiness she had left, while she seemed to be his greatest regret. Something he had to repent for. He'd spent the weeks since his death changing for the better, joining the clerisy and giving up the family vices that'd haunted him all his life, growing so much warmer and kinder for it. Meanwhile, she was the specter at his back, keeping him anchored to a past she couldn't stop drowning in. What should she have expected from a town where nothing stayed buried?

If she were gone, perhaps they could both find true peace.

Friede asked, "Would you take it back, if you could? If you found me dead in the lake again."

He lowered his head. The lashes closest to his freshly wounded temple had begun to drain of color, flashing against his cheek like fresh snow.

"I don't know," he said. "I know what I want. And I know what would be right."

She heard the next part unspoken: *But they aren't the same thing.*

Friede's knees shook, strength leaving her slowly. She clung to his hands, afraid she would sink through the floor otherwise, down into the dark with all the old bones and Eluned's silent screaming corpse.

"I love you too," she said softly, because it was the only truth she was still sure of in the moment. She stroked his knuckles with the tips of her fingers. *I wish that was enough to fix things*, she thought, but couldn't say.

The warmth of his answering smile and now thawed something inside her. She nudged his shoulder until he finally lay on his side, jostling the cat from the pillow. "Just rest now." After a moment, she added, "The past is dead. Let's bury it and move on." It came out hollow and wishing.

"Is that really what you want?"

Friede sighed. "I don't know."

"Tell me what you want. Anything."

She smiled, small and rueful.

She wanted him. And she wanted to be gone. And she knew there was no having both.

Friede couldn't bring herself to answer. Amid her dithering, the only sound in the room was Moira's breathing as the cat's ears perked, and she slunk from the bed to the floor. A low, warning sound rumbled in her throat. Friede looked to the cracked door, listening.

Footsteps. Light and lilting on the stairs.

By the time she coaxed herself to turn, it was too late to catch the intruder by surprise.

Friede's mouth fell open as Julius Delvin, a shade paler than when she'd seen him last, walked calmly in and shut the door behind him.

CHAPTER EIGHT

DEAD MAN WALKING

The snowdrop in the pocket of his vest had died. The stem was a brittle black, petals curling like fingers on a withered hand. Friede stared at it as he stepped into the room: an impossibility. A miracle, her tired mind corrected. He trod so light, so carefully, not even disturbing the dust.

Friede heard herself call out, "Julius?"

He hesitated a moment, then smiled. The gray skin around his eyes crinkled audibly.

Friede's relief swept her away for a moment, and she forgot about Lor, Eluned — all the confusion sickening her thoughts since morning. She didn't know what it meant for Delvin to be here, awake after the rites had failed and with Death's skull missing.

It was still Allhallowsmas. It seemed inappropriate to interrogate a miracle.

"Friede," he said in a choked voice. "You look well."

Bast gasped something wordless behind her. His fingers brushed her trousers, but the weak grip barely registered. Friede stepped forward.

"When did you wake?" she asked.

He mimicked her, steps shaky but sure. In one of his eyes, all the tiny vessels branched into a mesh of red. She hadn't noticed earlier; perhaps he had been ill after all. Sore regret plucked at her heartstrings for not calling on him since his retirement.

He outstretched a vein-webbed hand, and Friede took it, the skin papery under her touch. His other hand closed atop hers, barely applying pressure, but it made dark spots bloom across his wrinkled knuckles like dabs of watercolor.

She looked back into his face, searching more intently this time. She knew all too well how clumsily some wore their bodies after resurrection, how agonizing the slow return of mind and memory could be. There was life in the dead man's blood-addled gaze, certainly, but try as she might Friede could not find the friend she knew.

Her grip twitched involuntarily. "Julius?"

"No," answered the corpse finally. "I'm sorry."

The voice was ragged but still gentle, with a hint of Julius Delvin's rasp. But the accent didn't sit quite the same in the mouth, the smile around it ill-fitting as his funeral suit. Friede drew her hand slowly and carefully back. He made no move to stop her. She watched him, senses sharpening with her fear, until the pieces finally snapped into clarity, and she froze where she stood.

It was those eyes.

Behind the broken vessels, they were bright as flint. Friede knew them as well as she knew the blue, watery cold etched into her veins. Even in a man's head. Even wrapped in the face and clothing of a friend.

They were Lor's eyes. They gleamed with the same brightness as when she'd interrupted her witching-hour prayers by the lake.

The river lurched in her lungs.

The corpse, which no longer belonged to Julius Delvin, reached for her again. They took a tentative step forward, and the floor blackened under their feet as if with creeping damp.

She didn't want to believe it, but it was impossible to do anything but believe. The truth stared right through her from Julius Delvin's drooping blue eyes.

Friede's dead wife took hold of her chin, bruised fingertips gentle. Affectionate, almost. As if she meant to kiss her cheek or wipe away a tear, as if no time or pain at all stood between them. Like that moment by the lake had been nothing but one of her midnight terrors.

Friede glanced helplessly at her cane, where it rested against the bed. Within arm's reach, but only if she could make herself move. If she could summon the courage to fight the woman she loved. Her murderer.

This was not Lor's soul's true home. It wouldn't hold her. It shouldn't. Even with her faith in Death and their laws grave bound, Friede trusted that much.

Still, she hesitated.

That knife in her chest twisted, and she stayed hopelessly, deathly still as Lor stroked her cheek with stolen hands.

Bast moved for her.

"Get the fuck away from her," he croaked from the bed. He sounded ill, as ill as she felt, but hearing him gave her strength.

"Stop," she said. It came out barely a whisper. It was all she had the spine for.

Lor only said again, *"Friede."* The voice creaked from Julius Delvin's throat like it might have been an instrument carved of old, raw wood. "I missed you."

The words rang like a slap to her cheek. Even more shocking was the longing with which Lor spoke her name. This phantom who'd stolen the last breath from her lungs and left her in the cold had done the same to Eluned, and maybe to Julius Delvin too. People she knew. Innocent people.

Friede's fear froze over. She jerked, smacking the hand aside. Shaking, she found her cane and raised it like a sword. Against dead flesh, it might as well be.

"How ..." She struggled to form the words. "How are you here?"

Lor cocked her head to the side; the tendons rippled and strained beneath Delvin's starched collar. There were no dark fingermarks on his throat, at least. Her gaze slid off of Friede and landed heavily on Bastian.

"*Praise All-Eternal-Death who restores life to the dead*," she intoned, mockery twisting the words. Then she prompted, "Ask him, love. He knows. Ask him what he made me."

Love. Another twist of the knife, making her flinch.

Friede shook her head, not understanding, afraid to look away.

Bast's hand brushed against hers. He shifted in her periphery, groaning as he dragged himself up to sit.

"You shouldn't be here," he muttered. "You shouldn't fucking be here."

Syrupy old blood dribbled from the corner of Lor's lip. "I only took back what was mine."

Friede fought for words and came up empty. Bast struggled to his feet behind her, nearly toppling them both in the process. He clutched at Friede's arm like he meant to wrench it from the socket.

She glanced to him. "What does that mean?"

Bast ignored her. "Get out. You don't belong here, whatever the fuck you are. Get *out*."

Friede searched Bast's face desperately. Expecting fear, she found instead a distant kind of rage, then disgust, and, like Kamil, guilt flashing poisonous behind it all.

It felt like a betrayal to say, but she'd lost control of her tongue. "What did you do?"

He gritted his teeth instead of replying.

"Bastian."

He avoided her gaze like it was a wound. Friede let her grip fall and turned back to Lor, her nerves fraying, dread mounting. Her wife stood in the same darkening spot of floor, face almost placid.

Fighting to keep grounded amid the waves of dread washing over her, Friede pressed, "What have you done with Death's skull?" She brought the tip of her cane to Lor's chest. At the pressure, the flesh made a squelching, mud-like sound and gave just as easily. "Please ... if you ever loved me, tell me. *Please*."

Lor had the audacity to look hurt, but still shook her head. "Him first. A confession for a confession."

Bast's hands were in his hair, tearing at his curls. "You're supposed to be gone," he muttered.

Friede barely recognized him like this. She fell away a step, trying to get him back in the right light, but only succeeded in backing herself into a corner.

After a moment, Lor filled the space she'd emptied, coming nose-to-hollow-nose with Bast as another wound unraveled the skin of her cheek. She decayed before their eyes. Bast tried to shrink back against the bed, arm extended to grasp at the throat of Delvin's vest.

"Look at me," Lor groaned. "Or are you too much of a coward to face what you've done?"

He fought against her for a moment, but they remained tangled like the strangest of dance partners, neither seeming to have the strength to deal the other real harm. Friede watched, unsure of who frightened her most.

"Fucking monster — you killed her. You're a murderer," Bast spat uselessly.

Lor made a wet and shuddering sound. Friede thought it might have been a laugh; it sounded nothing like she remembered. "Does it disgust you then," she rasped, "that we're now the same?"

A calmness descended over Friede. She thrust her cane out. It struck Lor — and Julius — in the shoulder, sending her back several steps, then to her knees. Bast shrugged free of her grip and came to Friede's side, wavering on his feet. She put her arm out to stop his advance just the same. She didn't look into his face as he did it, too focused on the words that had left Lor's lips. The many wounds written in her stolen flesh each seemed a laughing mouth, mocking her horror. Mocking them all.

Managing to hold herself somewhat upright, Lor turned her dripping gaze to Friede. "I was dying," she said.

"What?" Friede's voice was small.

"It was fate that I made it as long as I did. After the rubble, the bombs, I was sick. I came home. Don't you see, love? It had to be fate." Friede did not see, but Lor wouldn't stop wheezing out the words. "I was going to save us both. If it hadn't been for him, I could have done it. Death would have heard me, and I could have struck a better bargain. I know it."

"Shut up," Bast heaved. Friede silenced him with a glare.

Blood, black in the dim light, dribbled down Lor's chin as she smiled. "I was never going to leave you dead, Friede. I found it here, finally, the secret to eternal life — true eternal life — not the flimsy resurrection this town loves. It's right there, in the rites. *In love there is no end.* Death's own words. How could they not heed their own words? You are my greatest love, Friede. The only love that hasn't been taken from me. I had to offer you."

"Stop!" Friede surprised herself at how her voice rang. She grasped her cane with both hands until her knuckle bones strained against the flesh. Her skull throbbed with all the tears she wanted so desperately to shed.

Lor's words should have meant nothing. She should have brushed them aside as the mania of an unholy, undone mind, something never meant to cross back through the veil. Instead, they opened a pit in her chest, dark and deep. It took all the strength she had left not to chase those horrible, rose-colored words into it.

In love there is no end.

Eternal life.

My greatest love.

"A woman is dead!" Friede howled. She speared Bast with her eyes. "Is it true? You — you had something to do with this?"

He seemed paler than usual, a much fresher corpse. He finally looked at her, drawing closer, and answered in a slow, trembling voice, "I did it for you."

Through teeth, she demanded, "Bastian Ruz. Look at me."

He did. Hopelessly, ruefully, as if she'd grasped him by the soul. His fists clenched and unclenched.

"Tell me."

"I ... I killed her. Because she killed you." His palms were splayed out, supplicant. "But I don't know how this happened, Friede. Truly, I don't."

"I don't care," Friede said, her voice broken. She wanted to shriek or rend her hair. Instead, she gestured to the bleeding, festering, stolen corpse before them. "Make it right."

She stepped away, legs threatening to buckle and send her to the floor beside her wife. As she skirted around her, Lor looked up with bitterness glowing incandescent behind her eyes, smothering the affection that previously flickered there in red.

The fight seemed to leave Bast. He sank back down to the bed. Through the gap in his fingers, Friede saw his eyes shut tight in quiet anguish, regret, or shame. She found she had no pity left for any of them.

All these lies weighed her down; she couldn't stand spending another minute in this room, drowning in them.

"You kept one piece," said Lor. "Tell me where to find the rest of me." She drew her hand to the pocket of Delvin's yellow vest and came out holding a small ring to the light, a shard of bone winking from its center.

Bastian's ring.

"You didn't." Friede looked to Bast again, but he only lowered his head further, dragging her stomach down with him.

She remembered his words from the lake. *I picked out the bone myself.* Her throat cramped in revulsion.

How many times had Bast said the rites while wearing a piece of Lor's corpse like some sick trophy? Ten times? Fifty? She'd been there every time. And each utterance was like a drop of blood in water, pulling a marooned soul apart, piece by torturous piece until it became something monstrous.

"The Pallwood," Bast said finally. "Just past the edge of town."

Friede shook her head. The dead couldn't travel past town limits ... when the ground was hallowed.

But now?

Bast must have seen her hope, because he said, "It's not like you think. We're not free. Tonight, at sunset, when the veil's undone ... without the hallowing, we'll just ... fade." He glanced to Lor darkly. "All of us."

Fade.

Fade to nothing, stuck in that empty in-between forever, until they forgot themselves entirely, forgot what it was to think or feel. No peace. Just dark and endless nothing.

She'd tasted it before. No one deserved that fate. Friede's legs began to shake.

Lor coughed, snapping her attention back to the moment. "It's fortunate, then," she said, "that I have our merciful Angel's skull." Dark blood frothed from her mouth. "You can have it once I have my body back."

Friede wanted to defy her, to have the last word. Bast looked like he wanted to commit another murder despite his crumpled posture. But there was nothing they could do.

Bast relented without looking at either of them. "There's an old oak tree with a heart-shaped knot in its trunk, just outside of town. You're buried under it."

Friede shut her eyes against a surge of nostalgia, tinged bitter now. She and Bast used to climb that particular tree as teenagers. She doubted her leaden limbs could do so much as lift her to one of the lowest branches now.

"I'll meet you there," said the corpse on her knees.

She looked last to Friede, gaze softening. But before she could speak again, her mouth wrenched open wide with a sound like fingers knifing through mud. Lor bent double, hacking, until fouled blood gushed and stained the front of Julius's funeral suit. The corners of the corpse's mouth split from the strain. Then the neck gave, wilting open in several places, the weight of the head bending the body in half at the waist. Only when the skull parted the skin and burst free, gray matter suppurating from its cavities, did the rest of the body of Julius Delvin slip, liquid and boneless, to the blackened floor.

CHAPTER NINE

RIGOR

The catacombs were quiet.

Eluned's body lay in her bed; the sheet covering her drooped with dark and purpling gore. There was, apparently, nowhere else to put her. No place of greater respect than the dusty little room she'd called home and where she'd spent every moment aside from funerals, cherishing a creature that didn't love her enough to save her.

Friede pulled the sheet away and let it fall. She made herself look.

Eluned's feet were bare and dirty. The hallowing was meant to keep corpses soft and ripe for resurrection for days on end, but Eluned was ashen and stiff. Blood soaked the wrinkles of her face and the front of her funeral-white robes, so much that it hadn't dried yet. It filled her open eyes, clouding their original clear-day blue. The kind of blue that so rarely graced Cairney's sky.

Whether a casualty of war or home-bred cruelty, this carnage was so foreign it skewered Friede to her core. It was simply wrong to see Eluned like this, nothing but a barren shell.

This was what the Angel of Death meant to protect them from.

Her fingers drifted to the dark marks on Eluned's neck. She still felt the grip of those same hands on her own skin. A death like that wasn't quick. It crept over you, vein by vein, bleeding hope dry. Friede would never forget that slow, icy drip of knowing her last moments had come, at the hands of the woman she loved, and they would be agony.

The last thread of her resolve snapped. With careful, trembling hands, she shut Eluned's eyes and mouth, wiping at the crusted blood until it transferred to her fingers.

"I'm so sorry," she whispered. It felt necessary to say. Someone owed Eluned that much.

She'd come here after fleeing Bast's room. Friede hadn't known what to do. Only that she couldn't bear to look at him or Julius Delvin's corpse for another second, and her legs had done the rest of the work, carrying her down to where the old bones slept. To where there was no one living left to lie to her.

Eluned, at least, had always honored her with honesty. Her kindness came without strings or the expectation of piety. When Friede had finally recovered and gathered the mettle to park herself at Eluned's door for counsel after her resurrection, the old woman had only asked her if she had any questions.

Friede, scoffing, had replied, "What could you possibly know that I don't?" She almost stood and turned back there and then. But bitterness had prompted her to add, "You're not the one who's dead. You're locked in a little room."

Eluned had said simply, "You're locked in your body," seeing right through her artifice. Then she asked, "What do you miss the most?"

"Tears," Friede answered instantly. Not only was she dead, but her grief was locked and bound away, too. She had no escape from herself. "And sleep," she added.

"Dreams?"

"No. Just sleep. I never liked my dreams," Friede admitted to her quietly. She couldn't remember the number of times she'd crept to her sleeping parents needing comfort after a nightmare, even into her teen years.

"There's a blessing in that," Eluned replied. They continued like that for a while, until Eluned had said, "I'm tired now — will you stay another day and see me again tomorrow?"

And Friede had. Until another day became another week, and she'd found more reasons to stay. She still came back to sit by Eluned's door and offer the litany of her griefs and questions, large and small, and Eluned listened. She had a surprising perspective for one locked so long in isolation. She'd never judged. Never shared the scraps Friede had fed her, those secret words she felt she couldn't speak in the sanctuary above.

She missed that honesty now more than ever.

The stone and earth dampened most of the sound from the church above, leaving Friede alone with her thoughts. There was no quieting the bitter memories gnashing their teeth in her head, no rest from the grief that gorged on her. No hiding from the wet rasp of Lor's voice promising that she loved her still.

In love there is no end.

The words burned.

She'd sounded so certain. Friede was helpless to wonder if Bast hadn't found her, would she have succeeded?

She was right, the words were there in the rites. With enough desperation behind one's eyes, they might have made a twisted kind of sense. Perhaps the Angel could be convinced a second time to change the rules of life and death.

But if it was true — if the secret to genuine immortality, and not walking death, was to offer up the ones you loved — was it really worth the price?

To Lor, it had been.

That was all that should have mattered. And yet.

And yet, she wondered. With tearless sobs plucking at her throat, she wondered. If Lor had told her that night what she hoped to achieve, would she have believed her?

That old Friede, the one who believed in miracles, was dead and gone. Buried in dark water.

Friede balled her hands into fists and willed the memories away, the bitter and the sweet, but the cloying weight of death clung to her no matter where she looked.

She thought of Bastian and had to bite down the urge to scream.

How long had this lie hung between them? This crime. How many smiles and jokes had it been hiding behind? Why had he not told her?

He did it for you, a traitorous part of her whispered.

Friede wondered when he'd stopped seeing her as the headstrong, steel-spined woman she knew herself to be, and instead saw someone he needed to shelter. She'd never asked for a knight. She'd certainly never asked for revenge.

He was a coward. Just like Lor, a coward hiding a bloody secret, and it disgusted her.

But she disgusted herself just as much.

They all had secrets. She hadn't told him her plan to abandon him until the option had been swiped from the table, the very day she meant to take her leave.

They were both cowards. Perhaps they deserved each other.

But the rest of Cairney didn't deserve what their cowardice had unburied.

Friede glanced down to Eluned again, still and silent. She gently grasped her hand and tried to find comfort in the solid press of their fingers locked together. Instead, anger flooded her, an icy wash that carried the horror to the margins of her mind until only chilled steel remained.

Instead of curses of blasphemy, the rites scored her tongue. She dropped shakily to her knees, still clutching Eluned's hand, and spoke low in the sepulchral air.

"Sleeper, wake," she muttered. "Great-Winged-Death hears and sees you this day and every day forevermore. Here you are offered a death without sorrow. Be at peace, for the merciful one beyond all human name and order grants you rebirth. Never must you mourn, for — for ..." Her throat spasmed. Friede forced the words out through gritted teeth, "For in love there is no end. Wake, sleeper. Wake. Please. Please wake."

She didn't trust the words. But that wasn't the point. It was ritual, a belief as old as the bones in the walls. She'd lived in Cairney long enough to know the power that held. Power *she* held.

Why shouldn't the Angel heed her call?

She needed music.

Friede clung to her wavering hope as she climbed the stairs out of the dark, bone dust swirling at her heels. The nave doors sat open as if expecting her. A few errant snowdrops drooped on the empty plinth where Julius Delvin lay hours earlier. She could see now the evidence of his profane resurrection in a sparse trail of papery, withered petals leading to the doors, a damp handprint on the back of a pew. The stones of the floor were stained in spots as if they'd bled.

So much decay left in her wife's wake.

Anger flared in her again, thinking of Julius's smile, his gentle mannerisms, his blackened teeth spilling rot. His head striking the floor. Her old friend's body was blighted ground now, too far gone for resurrection.

She had to stop this however she could. Before any others suffered the same fate.

Friede gingerly placed a snowdrop in her hair and sat at the piano. The requiem sprang to her fingers. She repeated the rites like lyrics between the notes, holding Eluned in her mind, holding her grief like a lantern against the dark, an open-handed offering.

I am your herald, Death. Answer me.

"Sleeper, wake," she chanted.

Friede played again and again, pounding her rage into ebony and ivory until her fingers went numb. Her song never erred. It was a perfect offering.

"Wake, sleeper, wake. *Please.*"

Friede waited, listening, hoping. Her hands fell still. Even the wind had gone silent and given up its restless beat against the church walls.

She felt nothing.

Nothing but the dread, creeping along her spine. Cold fingers at her throat, weeds and mud tangled about her ankles. Silence rushed over her. A vast, deafening silence, like a tomb inside her, shut and locked, and its key buried deep.

Death had not heard her.

When had the Angel of Death ever cared what she wanted? They'd left thousands of prayers unanswered. This was no different.

Why had she expected mercy now, after everything?

Friede curled her hands into fists and slammed them into the keys, crying out in frustration. The sound ricocheted off stone and returned to her in a mocking echo. Mocking her failure, her hope, her grief.

Even Death had abandoned them this time. She would have to see things through herself.

She was alone.

Until she wasn't.

Sensing a presence, Friede turned to find Kamil Kant standing on the stained floor, shivering in Bast's too-big coat. Their hair was a windswept tangle, both eyes red-rimmed as they watched her intently.

"What are you doing?" Kamil asked.

She smoothed her hands across the keys apologetically. "Praying, I suppose."

Slowly, they approached the piano, eyes widening with wonder as they drew closer.

"This is the biggest piano I've ever seen," they said, fingers coming to rest on the desk.

Friede shifted to the side of the bench, offering them a section to sit. They took it instantly, slim fingers running across the keys with reverence. When she started to play, her movements were smooth and confident, and the requiem that rang out was as perfect as Friede could ever hope for. She basked in the music for a moment, eyes shut, until Kamil's playing petered out without warning.

"I don't know what to do," they said, voice shaky and hushed, almost swallowed in the echo. "It wasn't supposed to be like this."

"I know." Friede found herself sounding surer than she'd expected, replying, "I'm going to fix it."

Kamil shook their head. "How?"

Friede stood from the piano and scanned the windows as snow began to fall. First, it came in gentle spirals, then the wind picked up, and the air blurred with swirling fat flakes. "First, I have to dig up Lor's grave."

If the declaration shocked Kamil, they gave nothing away. They just nodded and wiped a jittery hand across their face. Their fist came away with a streak of blood. Without a word, Friede drew the pale shroud from her coat and offered it out. It would serve the living better than the dead now.

Kamil took the shroud and wiped at their face shamelessly. "I'm coming with you."

Friede had dealt with enough teenagers in teaching to know refusal would only waste time and words. She nodded, smiling a slight and soft smile, and buttoned her coat high.

"All right. Let's go then," she said, offering Kamil her hand. "Daylight's fading."

CHAPTER TEN

BEYOND THE VEIL

Word of Cairney's fast-approaching fate must have finally sieved through the church walls, because there were no more coaches to catch when they reached the street, and they lost the better part of an hour making the trudge across town.

The sky had dimmed to the color of fresh bruised skin by the time Friede's boots broke the crusted snow that swallowed the path into the Pallwood. The trees snatched at the pair as they went, bony white claws catching on sleeve and hair. Fried clutched her scarf high and tight to her throat like it could keep her soul a secret from the gnashing wind. They only had to beat the dark.

Kamil kept pace, using the shovel they'd snatched from the churchyard as a walking stick to anchor each step in the deep snow.

When they paused a moment to shake the snow from their eyes, Friede said, "You know this isn't your fault, don't you?"

Kamil gave a scarcely audible laugh in return. "I offered to bring Lor the skull. No one twisted my arm."

"She didn't promise you anything if you followed through?"

A pause, filled by the wind. "Doesn't matter now," they muttered thickly. "I should've known better. She can't help me."

Friede wiped away the flakes that had gathered on her eyelashes and wouldn't melt. Even that small movement was hard-fought. "Help you find your parents, you mean?"

"I'm not daft," they said, speaking to the ground. "I know they're not coming back. Whether they meant to or not. I just ... got so tired of being lonely. I took my chance. What else could I do?" They shrugged, looking defeated.

Friede placed a hand on their shoulder, squeezing. "You did what you could to make it worth living another day. I understand."

Eventually, Kamil looked up at her through their long, dark lashes, nodding but saying no more. They kicked their boots together and took up walking again, offering her an elbow for support, which Friede took gratefully.

They moved quicker after that, the minutes passing in near silence save for the wind's rough blustering. It whistled through the trees in a discordant tune that rose and fell like distant laughter. Every once in a while, they passed what resembled a set of tracks in the snow: sometimes a hands-and-feet crawl, other times long, dragging steps that could have been nothing or anything.

To Friede, though, it seemed the same chaos that had been projected onto her eyes when she stood in the stairwell on Mausoleum Row. She tried to imagine what it must have felt like to be so barely there that not even the wind could hold her up, crawling dizzy miles through the trees in a form wrought of only deathless grief. Even now, with the ground no longer hallowed, it was difficult to make their way through so many of those hateful white trees.

Friede knew it would have been agony to make that crawl. She felt no satisfaction at that fact, no hint of righteous indignation. Just tired, same as she always felt. She had to trudge on.

The bony ends of the oak's branches came into view before they reached the top of the hill. Kamil paused just before they crested, fingers digging into the fabric of Friede's coat. It could have been the dying light glancing off the snow, but they looked ashen suddenly, bloodless. And for a moment, Friede feared they were going to leave her, turn back to town, find some warm place to hide and wait out the coming oblivion same as the storm. Friede clutched them back tightly, the bones in her fingers creaking loudly.

She didn't want to do this alone. They were so close now, she didn't think she could bear to let go.

Kamil only whispered, brows knit close and low over their eyes, "Do you hate Lor, for what she did?" They looked the barest bit bashful. "I've heard the clerics talk about you two."

Friede frowned. She tried to parse the intention between the words, whether it was fear or doubt or something else entirely, making their voice waver, Kamil's expression was inscrutable.

The answer slid from her lips without resistance, like when she'd coughed up weeds for hours after drowning. "I suppose I do."

Kamil nodded, and a thick feeling lodged in Friede's throat. She swallowed around it.

"But I love her too," she said. "I don't think I'll ever stop loving her." Her heart was a muddled thing, beaten and bruised and bleeding across her insides in shades she couldn't quite name or separate from each other. It didn't matter now. Grief leeched everything to gray in the end, even her loathing and love.

The wind clawed at their still bodies. Friede turned, hoping her tall frame could serve as a bulwark. A bright ruby dab of fresh blood rolled from Kamil's nose and dropped to the snow.

She gave a small smile. "It doesn't make any sense, does it?"

"No," Kamil answered. "But I get it."

Friede thought for a moment she saw the child's eyes go watery, but it could have simply been the cold.

She straightened up from the hunched position the wind had forced her to curl into and turned back to the last stretch of hill leering over them. Before she could ask if Kamil was ready to continue, they tramped ahead and began climbing, blinking hard. Friede followed, her legs all the more stubborn now for having rested a spell. The snow came down in volleys. It blurred the trees, blurred the sky, blurred the moment they crossed Cairney's edge into nothing but a blank haze.

There wasn't even a change in the air when they passed over. No trace of the hallowing to hold them back from oblivion or the cruelty of the cold hills. It was the sight of the old oak spiderwebbing out of the gray that finally marked how far they'd come. It stood just as tall as Friede remembered, bark pocked with what, as an adolescent, she thought were bullet holes, though the more likely culprit was hungry woodpeckers.

As children, she and Bast truly thought they might touch a cloud if they managed to reach the very top of one of those branches. Neither of them had ever proved brave enough to try in front of the other. ("I'm not breaking my neck on a dare," was her excuse to Bast. To which he'd replied, confident as anything, "Don't worry, I'd save your soul.")

There were no ominous ripples in the air to spell the presence of her murderer, no gouges in the snow except hers and Kamil's. Perhaps they'd already been covered over by the storm.

Kamil shivered against her side. If she still lived, their grip on Friede's arm might have bruised to the veins. She couldn't blame them; she shook nearly just as hard, standing in the shadow of her childhood, of oblivion.

Lor's name sat frozen on her tongue. Instead of calling out for her, she put her back to the wind and stared in the direction of town, searching for the strength to do what needed to be done. Just over the hill she spotted a figure in black shearing through the snow-choked distance, barely visible against the damson dark of dusk.

She knew Bastian by his shape, by his particular lumbering gait. But more than anything else she knew him by instinct, by trust, the same way she trusted her fingers to know their place on piano keys.

Of course it was him. No one else loved her so stubbornly. So completely.

The relief that lanced through Friede's chest didn't surprise her. Her previous anger seemed such a faraway thing, hollowed-out and buried as spring under snow. She gasped when she saw him, as if feeling the nerves in a severed limb come alight again. If her eyes were capable, she would have cried. The desperate want of it clawed at her sockets.

Bast's steps were surer than when she'd seen him last, though his skin had lost its pigment from brow to cheekbone, bleeding his edges into snow and sky. His black robe whipped to and fro as the wind rose and waned. He clutched a shovel of his own.

Friede grinned, though she shook. Coming closer, he grinned the same.

He was still a coward, still a liar, but so was she. Not even Death could break them.

Friede didn't know what she wanted to do most, but after some consideration, she placed a hand on his arm when he reached her side, holding tight like she held to Kamil. So many clumsy words stopped up her throat. She hoped that one small touch could convey what her tongue couldn't, what she was still too weak and frightened to voice.

Bastian, with his beautiful, honest face, smiled like she'd just conjured an early spring. It amazed her how he could still smile like that after all they'd put each other through. After today.

Heedless of her restraint, the wind blew harder, goading. Friede's resolve bent, then Bast reached back for her, and she didn't resist. She pitched forward and embraced him. His shovel clattered unceremoniously to the snow as he wrapped his arms around her middle and held tight. Friede wanted nothing more than to hide in the sturdy circle of his arms and rest. The instinct was as foolish as it was impossible.

She touched his cheek. "I missed you. And I'm sorry."

"Me too." He took her hand and kept up that small but brilliant smile. Quietly, just for the two of them, he said, "It kills me, you know, whenever you're not with me. I've been a fucking fool."

Friede wanted to laugh, but her throat was too tight to make more than a whisper. "I think I have too."

"You've earned a little foolishness, I say."

"I don't forgive you," she said. She had to say it, while they still had time.

He stroked her cheek. "I don't want you to."

The snow beside them crunched as Kamil shifted from foot to foot.

Bast pried his gaze away from her face with considerable effort and nodded toward them. "Here to help?"

"Nothing better to do," they replied, lips running red.

Bast touched the frayed end of Friede's scarf, his gaze softly questioning. She nodded, and he slipped the scarf from her neck and offered it to the child. "You're going to need this."

Kamil hesitated but took it. Their eyes flicked down to the handprints bruised into Friend's neck. She resisted the urge to cover herself. They were a testament to exactly the kind of woman Lor was, behind all the promises, the beautiful, blushing smiles, and reckless idealism.

Friede didn't want any more illusions. If Lor watched from somewhere hidden in the haze, let her see what she'd done. If death had left any shred of a heart in her, perhaps she'd feel some guilt. Perhaps, she'd let this end without any more suffering.

Kamil tucked the scarf around their face and nodded their thanks, then reached into their pocket and drew out Bast's ring, glinting with its weathered chip of bone.

"It was sitting on my pillow when I ran back to the church. Like Lor knew I planned on finding you again."

Blank-faced, Bast slipped the ring onto the finger of his full hand, then gave Kamil's shoulder a soft pat. "Thank you. I'm glad you came back."

"You've had to chase me down too much already," they huffed. "Sorry."

Bast shook his head, then led on toward the trunk of the old oak. He cleaved the blade of his shovel into the ground beneath, hard enough his thick arms bulged in their sleeves.

"Right here," he said. "This is where I buried her."

Friede followed him. She waited until he looked her in the eyes. "Tell me."

CHAPTER ELEVEN

A GHOST STORY

I was drunk off my ass, as far as I remember. That's not an excuse. I just mean it's foggy.

You know my dad always said I'd die a drunk. We have that in common, I guess. Maybe that's what you get when you spend your whole life brewing gin ... I think that was how he wanted to go, at least, and wishing it on me was just his way of saying we were still family even if I never acted like the son he wanted. Your blood can catch up to you like that if you're not careful, I guess.

Sorry, I'm getting off track. I'll start from the beginning.

I found you early that morning, coming off a long night at Clay's. Looking back now, I think I saw Lor, too, on my way over. I thought it was her anyway, walking by the church, but I was never sure. I thought she'd be with you. But when I finally did get to the house, it looked like she'd run off, left all her things.

It was just a day or so later, maybe. You were back, but not really speaking to me or anybody, and I was trying to forget, or ignore, really, how angry I could tell you were — of course I could tell — and it made me angry, too.

So, I got pissed and I walked. I ended up further out of town than

I'd meant to get, further than I'd ever really gone since we were kids. I thought I'd be alone. Thought maybe I'd die like dad, keep the family tradition going. I don't know.

But then she was there. Way out deep like I was, but I don't think she ever knew the woods like the rest of us do — not growing up with it and all. She must have gotten lost. She was out of her mind too, in real awful shape, frostbitten to hell and coughing her lungs out. But I guessed she was headed back to town.

Back to you.

It seemed like she was, at least. And I thought, well, fuck that. She doesn't get to come back here after what she did.

I swear I didn't start out meaning to hurt her. I told her to leave and never think about coming back, that she wasn't welcome in Cairney anymore, and you were better off without her. I thought she was already half dead and would be nobody's problem soon enough. If I just left her out there, she wasn't likely to be found, and the snow would take care of the rest. Then we could go back to how we'd been.

I told her again to go, and she just laughed at me. Her face all cracked and frozen bloody, leaving wild little tracks in the snow like some animal. She wasn't dressed for the cold.

"You didn't come to the wedding," was all she said. "Friede asked for you."

I hadn't; I remember that. I'd forgotten the date. Slept right through the whole thing. I know I never told you — you never asked. I didn't think you wanted to know. I'm sorry, but it was probably for the best. I would've been drunk, or at least hungover, and I know how you felt about that. I wouldn't have wanted you to be unhappy. I don't imagine it mattered in the end. But hey, you didn't come to my funeral, so I guess that makes us even.

That isn't fair, I'm sorry. You had your reasons.

Anyway ... I didn't think to try explaining any of this to Lor. I just asked what was so funny. She wouldn't stop laughing. It was fucking unsettling, and I kept talking to distract myself, but I remember what she said. It scared the hell out of me.

She said, "You all pray so hard for rot. You worship it. But it's everywhere. Your angel didn't save you; they're just the vulture that picks everything clean once the shelling is done. You beg and you beg and you beg enough so they'll agree to change the rules to their own game for a while. It's been done before. I've studied it all. Why not for me? I'm already rotting."

She was laughing and coughing so hard the words were shredded, but the last thing she told me was, "I'm coming back for her."

When I swung at her, I'd honestly forgotten I had the bottle in my hand. It shattered right off, and she might've been dead from that alone, not that I checked. I just kept swinging until I couldn't see her face anymore. Sorry — I'm not trying to be cruel. I just want you to know how it happened. What I was thinking.

And it was about you, but it was about more than that, too. Any bag of bones in town will tell you anything you could want to know about the war, but no one ever talked about it like she did. Who gave her the right, I thought. She just swept in here, never been to Cairney before, but talked like she knew us, knows Death like we do. I believed Death was better than that.

My parents never thought much of the church, I know. I really didn't either until they brought you back. I think ... that's part of the reason I got into the clerisy. I never told you that either, did I? But I wanted to prove her wrong.

Actually, I think it started with Eluned.

Don't laugh, but when I was a kid — real young — I had this cat that died. My first cat. Her name was Mari. She was my only friend for a long time, before you. Of course, she got old, and when she died, I brought her to Eluned to see if she could bring her back. I know now that's ridiculous, Death's gift is only for people, not pets, but Eluned didn't send me home. No, she sat me down and we said the rites together and waited for a miracle. Mari didn't come back to life, of course. But it meant something to me that she tried. It meant a lot. I never forgot that.

All that's to say, the real reason I wanted to work with the church was because it's not all about death. Not remotely. There's a lot more to it than funerals. It's easy to think that, but there's the shelter, and putting people up in places like Mausoleum Row, keeping people fed, just being good to people who need it. We bring people back when they want to be — yes, sometimes when they don't, I know, but I hope you know I'll never do that again if I can help it ... but we keep them alive, too. You never wanted to see that from your end.

So, I don't think Lor was right. She knew death, I'll grant her that, but she was wrong about *our* Death. They're not the one who saves us. It's us — you and me — and everyone alive and dead, doing whatever we can, like Eluned did for me. And if the Angel gives us all more time to give each other, then I think we should take it.

Sorry, that's not what you asked.

The rest is kind of a blur. I know I dragged Lor back here and buried her.

I took one of the bones from her hand so I'd remember once I sobered up, and put it in my ring when I joined the clerisy. That was the stupid part, I guess. Knowing what I know now. But I thought if I'd buried her outside of town, that would be the end of it.

I never told you any of this. I'd already fucked things up enough.

That's the story. I didn't say it wasn't gutless, but it's the truth.

But afterwards, I started having nightmares about it all, drinking even more so I could sleep, taking walks around town when I couldn't, you know. You remember what I was like. Now you know why.

That's why I'd been drinking the night I died. I didn't want to sleep, and Clay kicked me out, so I walked all up and down the river in the dark. Guess it'd started freezing by then. Must've slipped.

And, well, you know the rest.

CHAPTER TWELVE

WAKE

"So, it's your fault," Kamil said first, voice barely rising past the wind and the collar of their coat, but sharp enough to have Bast flinching. "What a mess."

He took the blow graciously and only nodded. "Drunk and bitter are a horrible combination. Let that be a lesson, I guess."

Kamil shook the snow from their hair. "I don't think I should be taking lessons from either of you. Sounds like you fucked everything up."

"Look. I'm an idiot, and an ass, I know. At least I'm not hiding from it anymore," Bast countered.

"So I've heard."

"Less bickering, more digging, please," Friede said. She leaned on her shovel and stared into the black, smiling crevice that had begun to form in the smothered earth. She jerked up when Bastian touched her arm, fingers light and testing.

"What?"

"Are you going to say something?" he asked.

Friede readjusted her grip. "What do you want me to say?"

He shrugged. "Anything." After watching her for a moment, he paced back to the opposite end of the grave and took up his shovel again.

Eventually, Friede said, "I never knew about your cat."

"Seriously, Fee."

"I mean it. I wish I'd known that earlier. About Eluned. She was ... such a good woman."

He only nodded.

She continued, "All that work. And you never breathed a word of it to me. Why?"

He didn't hesitate this time, though she could see the thorny shape of the words in his pinched mouth. "I was afraid to lose you."

Friede felt as if he'd stepped through ice and plunged into the deep, dark lake of her. It took a long time for the cold ebb of his words to settle. She dug her boots deeper into the snow and nodded slowly, sighing to herself.

"I was afraid to lose you too." She was hardly conscious of the words until they'd left her mouth. They poured out through the crack he'd made in her, a weeping wound. "That's why I never told you I wanted to leave until today. And why I didn't go to your funeral. It was too real, too terrifying. I needed you here. I still need you. You're the reason I'm ..." Her throat spasmed, and she couldn't finish.

Bast looked at her, wounded. He clutched his shovel tightly. "You don't have to worry about me, Friede. I'm not going anywhere." Finally, he sighed, relieved, and offered her a small smile. She couldn't help but mirror it, basking in the impossible warmth of him.

It felt odd, smiling while standing over a half-unburied grave as oblivion bore down on them from the bleeding sky. But it felt familiar too. After all the hours they'd whiled away as teens when they managed to trudge this far out, joking and talking about nothing of any consequence, hiding from the world down the hill that could be so cold.

When they'd talked of death here, it held none of the stark weight of reality. Like the war, they'd only known the negative space of it, the places it had chipped away at the mappable world's borders over time. This place was their oasis where the truth couldn't touch them. They used to laugh at Death here, pantomiming stiff-limbed headless horrors, anything to make the reality of their inevitable losses less frightening.

Bast's father was the first to go. They drank to him here, and huddled together sick afterwards. They held their own funeral for his mother three years later in the comfort of the Ruz home. Bast insisted she be buried in the churchyard, not the nonbeliever plot on the south edge of town; she'd been a faithful woman, just not in the Ċairney tradition. Volf relented only after Friede's parents had pressed the issue, but she'd heard a word from Eluned had tipped the scales.

Friede felt how acutely they'd both been weathered since leaving the shelter of these branches. She barely recognized herself now.

They resumed digging. The movement became comforting. Friede's arms turned numb, but she trusted her limbs to know their route, like when she played.

She cast her gaze to where Kamil had settled, hunched against the trunk of the oak to shield themselves from the deluge of snow. Their hands were splayed on their knees, fingers dancing as if over invisible keys. Friede recognized the notes as the ghost of a requiem, and smiled. Occasionally they huddled deeper unto their coat and glanced to the waxing grave, but gave no commentary, and wouldn't meet Friede's eye.

Returning to her digging, she said, "How did you manage it? Dredging everything up again."

Bast shrugged, hefting another shovelful aside. "It isn't easy. But it brought me back to you. Regretting that feels ... ungrateful."

"You think it's all fate then, do you?"

"Isn't it?" He flashed her a gleaming grin.

Friede opted not to reply. She struck deep again, and this time her shovel grazed something different that sent a tremor up her arms.

She grasped after the shovel as it fell, but her heel caught the slope at a rough slant, and she plunged several feet down, landing on her hands and knees in the dirt. When she pulled back, gasping, her fingers came away caked in brittle black and gray, too slick to be the texture of the abused earth under her.

Not weeds or roots. Hair.

"Oh," Friede choked. "Oh."

She didn't know whether she meant to cry out for help or to retch. Only a puzzled lump in her throat remained, not unlike the strands snarled around her hands.

She knew that hair well. Her fingers had brushed it the first time she and Lor kissed. She'd been charmed by it, the natural silver woven through the black, utterly unique to the white shocks that bleached the heads of the undead. They broke now in her grasp, fragile as snowflakes.

Bast called her name from above, but she didn't turn to him. Her hands sought the dirt again to follow those strands to their roots, hurriedly brushing clumps away until something shaped like a forehead emerged, the shell of an ear, the corner of an open, bloody eye. Growing frantic, Friede plunged her hands deeper and gasped when a shard of glass sliced a line across her fingertips. The flesh that winked out from the cuts was dark purple and bloodless, but it still shot her through with horror, and she flinched away.

"Friede," Bast said, suddenly at her side, his hand coming to enclose hers. His other came around to her forearm and tried to lift, but she was as frozen as the corpse at her feet.

"No, *no*," she snapped. "Let me see."

This was her wife. Or what remained of her before she'd become a monster.

She glared until Bastian's hands retreated. He knelt at her side, and after a moment's hesitation, began to brush the dirt away as she had.

Little remained of her face. The flesh left there resembled Friede's own: pale and bluish where it wasn't split, with no more of Lor's soft peachy coloring, just violet-tinged viscera shredded by amber glass.

A slurry of dissonant emotions rioted in Friede's chest. At the center, a stone weight of truth: *I loved you.*

I loved you; I love you, and you killed me, and look what's become of us.

Friede dug her hands into the dirt beside Bast's and excavated her wife's corpse from the confines of the frozen earth, working in slow handfuls until her sleeves were caked wet and brown. She focused carefully on that frostbitten sliver of her face, how it stared open and blank at the sky, the same hollow stare as her sleepwalking episodes.

Bast avoided it, but Friede couldn't look away. She felt compelled, in part, to make bare the violence to the remains of the daylight.

One of Volf's refrains sprang to mind: *a grave is a curse.*

She understood what he meant now. The hallowing had stripped the war's casualties of their graves and built the church from their bones. Since then, no true decay had dwelt in Cairney. They'd all been spared from it, like children with their ears cupped while adults spoke profanities.

In that respect, Death did seem merciful after all.

Careful of her fingers now, Friede plucked the glass from Lor's face. The lips she'd kissed were chapped and crusted in old blood, but mostly intact. The few, much shallower cuts might heal upon resurrection. Her hand lingered on her cold cheek.

"Should we say the rites?" she asked.

Even with his back halfway turned, she made out the sound of Bast's low and humorless laugh. "She's heard them more than enough times."

The wind picked up then, almost knocking Friede back. A dusting of snow swirled in the air, making dizzying patterns before her eyes.

She braced as the vision struck her, dropping lower to the ground to keep her balance as her sight wheeled and melted into white.

White snow on willow branches, white-blond hair, and white satin. Friede was staring at herself in her nightgown. Staring from

Lor's eyes while she lay dead in Lor's arms, her face gone blue and teeming with broken veins. She heard the ragged whisper of Lor's voice, rising and falling as she tried and failed to carry her up and out of the lake, split with sobs: "*In love there is no end. In love there is no end.*"

Then it was done. Friede caught herself falling forward into the grave, but as she tried to rise to her feet, a deep, retching sound erupted from the earth she'd planted her hands in, and frostbitten fingers latched around her wrist. The grip shocked a startled noise from her throat, and she went nearly limp with fear.

Lor's corpse twitched.

Friede's first stupefied thought was that resurrections in the church had never been so loud.

Again and again, that retching echoed in her skull and over the hill. Lor's mouth gaped and worked in wordless spasms as she spat out cakes of bloody earth and glass.

Friede shook and could do nothing but watch. She knew the power of death throes. One had to travel backward through them to achieve resurrection. She'd regurgitated mud and river water on the floor of the catacombs just like this. A second life only after a second death.

It was a cruel joke, calling that mercy.

After the initial tide of revulsion had passed, she nudged the shoulder of the corpse until she turned on her side, and the awful choking noise subsided somewhat. A kindness Friede wished she'd been offered during her own ordeal. Such small favors weren't the church's specialty, only spectacle. The only comfort was ritual.

Friede laid her hand over Lor's and began to hum a requiem. It was quiet and strained, but it was the best she had to offer.

Staring down at her now, she couldn't reconcile how this Lor was the same one who had held her thrashing by the throat underwater until she breathed no more. The same who'd vowed to spend life and death with her.

Friede watched her corpse unbury itself in fits and starts.

Watched and held on tight as Lor's fingers made a chorus of small cartilaginous cracks, never once letting go of her own. Her jerking and stiff-jointed straining was too grisly to watch, but Friede felt that she must, the same way she felt during funerals.

Someone ought to bear witness to the horror of this miracle. Someone ought to mourn the living dead.

There was little left of the square-jawed and coldly lovely face Friede knew. What came up from the dirt resembled wet, rotten paper stuck in a rictus of pain. Through the constellation of glass and wounds only one stark white eye remained to squint through the haze of snow. Friede didn't know whether she pitied Lor more like this, or as a monstrous wraith. Both were a tragedy.

Lor lurched up to sitting, her hand still clasped tight to Friede. She gave herself a stilted once-over, movements sluggish and lilting. Her chin craned up, and her gaze landed on Friede, then her mouth fell open in a long, wordless cry.

It had something of the howling wind in it, something of a lamb trussed for slaughter, something so unearthly even Friede couldn't name it. Her chest ached at the sound, though, and her fingers twitched with the itch to comfort, the loving instinct still not lost from her flesh though she'd been betrayed, and betrayed, and betrayed.

"I know, dear," she said, barely conscious of her jaw's working.

Groaning like a drunk, Lor tried and failed to rise to her feet. Glass crunched as she moved. It gleamed in her mouth when she tried to reply. She didn't appear to have a tongue left. In the end, she just grasped out for Friede. Friede let her come closer. And she let her own arms come around the bloody, wrecked remains of her wife.

She answered the groaning again with, "I know," because she did, and, "I'm sorry," because she was.

This was death. And it was a curse.

Lor tried again to reply. What came out sounded like a "no," though it was impossible to be sure. A single bloody tear dangled frozen under her eye, almost black in the dawning dusk. Friede placed her hand on her cheek and brushed the droplet aside, careful not to cut her fingers further.

Lor's gaze flickered away, sliding over Bast entirely, but landed on the old oak tree and Kamil beneath it. They hadn't moved through the entire unburying, but now shrugged the snow from their hair and came to stand at the head of the grave. Bast tried to keep them back, but they slipped under his arm as quick as an alley cat.

"Lor."

The utterance was not questioning, or kind, or even betrayed. It sounded utterly empty, like part of the wind, answering the call Lor had cast out.

Lor's hands groped at Friede's coat as she tried and failed again to speak. She was even more horrible to watch up close, yet Friede couldn't look away.

Perhaps that was why she hadn't seen the precise moment Kamil drew the knife from their coat.

CHAPTER THIRTEEN

UNFINISHED BUSINESS

Kamil descended into the grave with barely a sound, fitting snugly into the length of Lor and Friede's combined shadows. Their thumb pressed at the hinge of the pocket knife, and it came open with a click. Before Friede could utter a gasp, Kamil snapped their wrist, and the point of the blade flicked out to kiss the sunken skin below Lor's unblinking eye. One twitch and her end would come again.

"You told me you'd help me," they said, voice thick. "You left me."

"Kamil," Bast cried out. He teetered on his feet but didn't approach, eyeing Kamil with worry.

"Why should we help her?" they argued. Their breath shuddered through chattering teeth. "Why does she deserve it? *Why*?"

"She doesn't," Friede broke in. She thought of the fast-fading daylight and their hopes of salvation winnowing away with it. "It's not about her. Please, I know she hurt you — she hurt me too. Think about Eluned. Without Lor, we'll never get her back. And we'll lose so many more." One of her hands crept up toward the knife, imploringly.

"Kamil, this won't help you," Bast added, his hands outstretched and placating. He seemed so far away. "You don't want to hurt anyone."

"What do any of you know about me? You're just like her. Just a bunch of fucking ghouls haunting each other. You don't know anything. I'm not ... I can't end up like all of you."

"You're right. Haven't we all suffered enough?" Bastian pleaded.

Kamil choked back something sob-like and frustrated. Their grip tightened around the blade, sweat-slick despite the cold. Friede saw them inhale sharply; frantic, she didn't think, just reacted. She released Lor and reached up with both hands, and Kamil moved too, whether to strike or relent or something else, she didn't have time to find out before they collided.

Schlink, came the crisp, meaty rasp of metal through flesh. It was a startling sound.

Kamil jerked, whimpered, and jerked again. Friede jerked with her. Then a chorus of snaps, as brittle links of bone broke apart from their siblings.

It took Friede several moments to realize she could no longer feel much of her hands.

She'd stopped the knife from cutting into Lor. Stopped a second death.

Friede tried to count that as a blessing, but it felt impossible when she glanced warily down to see five fingers sitting between her and Kamil, a dirty robin's egg blue against the dirt.

Something like a gasp sputtered out of Friede, turning at the end to a warbling shriek. The loss was painless. That made it all the worse. Without the lurid blare to sharpen her senses, she felt barely present at all.

Like that moment in the catacombs, her skull rang with only one refrain.

No no no.

Kamil released the knife. It dropped to the earth soundlessly.

Friede thought she saw on Kamil's cracked lips that same futile litany: no, no, no.

Don't, Friede wanted to add to the chorus. But her lips wouldn't move, and as soon as they'd freed themselves of the knife, Kamil sucked in a trembling breath and scrambled back. They crested the side of the grave and ducked Bast's second attempt to halt them, tears frozen and twinkling on their cheeks.

"Don't." This time, Friede forced the word out. It echoed.

Kamil didn't seem to hear. They only glanced back once — at Friede, and Lor, and the grave — before turning and breaking into a run. They disappeared between the scarred trees, the haze of falling flakes eager to swallow them up.

"Fuck!" Bast shouted. He hurried after, steps stumbling, before remembering himself and turning back to Friede. His face creased with horror a moment later, as Lor unsteadily picked up the knife from the snow.

Friede was still frozen with shock, staring at the shred of flesh that kept her dangling pinky finger attached to the rest of her hand.

No no no.

Friede forced her gaze aside. She locked onto Lor's mangled face. Despite the carnage, she looked utterly human in that moment. And so afraid. Waking from a deep, dreadful dream.

Lor pressed the pearly hilt of the knife into one of Friede's hands, the one that had the most fingers left. Then, gently and trembling, she moved that hand by the wrist until the point of the blade grazed the flesh over her heart.

"No," Friede choked, the word a shattered thing.

Lor's grip tightened once, a false pulse, a plea.

Please. Her blackened lips caressed the word.

"Where is it — the skull?" It was Friede's turn to beg, now. "Please tell me. I can still save us."

Another bloody tear worked its way down the valleys of Lor's cheek. She shook her head. Pressed Friede's hand harder until they both shook.

"Friede," Bast called from behind her, his voice urgent, almost cold. Slowly, she turned to him. The wind battered him on all sides. She didn't know how he stayed standing.

Lor's hand touched her chin, gently turning her face back. The frostbitten skin of her fingers was rough, like it might leave splinters. Friede's forehead came to rest against hers.

"Tell me," she pleaded again.

Lor's lips pulled into a broken half-moon of a smile. They formed the shape of another word at the same moment that her fingers brushed down the slope of Friede's jaw to her bruised throat. She flinched, and Lor heaved forward, and the knife went in so easily it didn't make a sound at all.

No.

That was the word.

One last fearful plea. One last insult to damn them all.

Friede choked on a cry. She held Lor there, frozen for a few painful moments, before her instincts kicked in and she wailed, shoving her back.

Lor was already limp. She dropped to the snow, her one eye lightless. Still Friede watched, waiting for movement.

A twitch, another groan, a ripple in the air, anything. But Lor was still, and within moments, snow started to gather on her corpse, blotting her out just like Bastian had wanted those few scant months ago.

She was gone. She couldn't be gone. Not after all they'd done to raise her, to appease her.

They'd come so close.

Friede's periphery was choked with snow. She and her dead wife seemed to be the only two creatures left in the world, suspended in the whiteout. Friede was tempted to stay there for however long she had left.

The wind howled. Something touched her shoulder.

A hand. Soft hands she knew well. Their gentle weight threatened to shatter her.

"What'd she say?" Bast asked.

Friede clenched her teeth against a sob.

"Nothing."

His only response was a sigh that the wind swallowed. "Fee," he said eventually, pressing more insistently at her shoulder. "We have to go after Kamil. They'll freeze out here. *Friede*."

She bit back another sob. At the sound of her name uttered so helplessly, at his closeness, at everything. She couldn't reply.

"She's gone," Bast said. The two words rang in the air, a death knell.

She shook her head no, no, no.

"I'm sorry."

"She can't be. She has to fix this."

"She can't help us, Friede. Her soul is bound in death now. We have to go."

Just leave me alone.

It would be easy, and cruel. And not what she wanted. Friede nearly said it.

"I can't," she cried. Bast's arms came around her more solidly, holding her against his chest. He managed to pull her up to standing. She went numbly, chest catching on breathless sobs. When he reached for her hands, the limp, mangled things, Friede pulled away. The pain and sympathy in his eyes were unbearable.

Without her hands, there would be no more music. That joy of her fingers dancing across the keys, the thrum in her bones. It was gone. Like her wife. Like the rest of her peace. Hacked off and buried in shrouds of snow. The spidering nerves were severed so she could barely summon a twitch in what remained. If she waited a thousand years, perhaps they might heal a touch. But she was not a tree. Her patience was finite.

Bast reached for her again, and this time she did not dodge his entreating hands. They grasped the sleeves of her coat with softness she surely didn't deserve. She knew how hard he'd fought to become so gentle. Fought mocking children, fought his history, fought the weight of Cairney's judgment like a millstone binding him at the ankles.

Bastian. Sweet Bastian. Ever at her side, loving twice as hard for all he'd been hurt.

Her last remaining love. She could at least try to spare him.

Friede drew her spine up straight. "I'll find Kamil."

"What?"

"Look." She summoned a small, empty smile and gestured with her chin. The trail of Kamil's petite footfalls wove deeper into the trees, leading south. Out of town. "It's almost sundown. Go back, please. Just let me go."

If by some miracle they could still be saved, it would be better if only one of them sacrificed themselves to the miles beyond.

Bast drew even closer. His brows knotted together and painted his face with shadowy longing. "Are you sure? That's what you want?"

"I can't have what I want. So, I'll settle for what's right," she said.

He looked as if she'd knifed him in the sternum. He only leaned closer still, and when he reached for one of her hands again, she let him take it. Bastian brought it to his chest and held it close over his heart. His beautiful bleeding heart. Then he pressed a kiss to the back of her palm.

"For luck, then," he whispered.

Friede smiled through the pain.

She wouldn't let herself promise anything, not with her limbs and spirit so weak, no matter how badly she wanted to. If she was damned, she refused to let her last act to him be a broken promise.

"For luck," she said, and brushed her lips once, lightly, to his cheek.

Before her mettle could crumble, before he could pull her closer and beg her to stay, before she could kiss him properly and whittle away into oblivion at his side, Friede pulled away.

But she held the image of his glittering, mismatched eyes in her mind, all the unspoken emotion he let smolder there. It gave her the strength to turn and scale the grave's edge, to follow the tracks left in the snow, until Bastian and the shape of the old oak blurred and dissolved into white, and Friede was left alone to trudge headlong into the storm.

CHAPTER FOURTEEN

THRENODY

Friede called Kamil's name into the roaring wind for as long as she had the strength. It became a prayer, answered only by its echo, though even that returned to her distorted, a thready mockery of her voice. She called until she felt something threaten to tear behind her leaden tongue. Then she only cursed, so quiet it made no sound at all.

She'd never ventured this far outside Cairney even as a child. The stories of buried bombs and bodies razed by guns the size of titans had cowed her as a young girl so much she could not wholly conceptualize the idea of a land beyond. She'd imagined instead bayonet blades peppering the earth like a field of thorns, streams running with endless red. In truth she contended mostly with the weather, which was treacherous enough without the hallowing to usher her tide-like in any one direction.

She was free. And she was damned.

The snow came up to her shins now, caking her legs. But Friede was familiar with heaviness, the kind that clung. And she wasn't afraid of the cold. It was the dark that worried her most. The arbor blotted what little sunlight remained from her vision. In perhaps an hour's time, all would be dark, and she had scant hope of finding her way back to town. Back to Bast.

What was one more love to grieve? She had so many already. They fell upon her like snowflakes. She was the eye of that storm.

Friede still mouthed Bast's name as the wind split the skin of her lips. It grew harder and harder to track the shape of Kamil's footprints as snow piled on and the shadows grew denser, the wind dragging the downy flakes every which way. A smattering of branches snagged on her coat, dropping lumps of snow, and Friede stumbled again, falling to her knees.

Beside her, blood dotted the snow. Just a small sprinkling, a drop here, another a few paces ahead, on and on until they disappeared in the shadow of a drooping tree.

Friede heard a sound then, mostly muffled by the wind. A very living sound. A ragged cough.

Looking harder now, she could make out a crouched shape by the trunk, nearly lost in the architecture of long shadows.

"Kamil."

The shape of Kamil Kant burrowed deeper into their coat and didn't speak.

Friede crawled on her knees to the tree. The snow clung to her thighs and middle but she was already dead, already frozen.

Kamil was in worse shape, sodden from head to toe and shivering mightily. A tumble in midwinter would do that to you, sapping the heat from your blood in no time. A quarter-hour more and they might have been lost too.

Friede tore the coat from her frame and held it outstretched. Kamil's dark eyes darted to her, but they made no move. They might have been too chilled to. Their face was blotched from crying. A stream of frozen blood snaked down their nose and teetered on their lip.

Friede came closer and did her best to drape the wool around their shoulders. "Please," she croaked. "There's no reason for another innocent person to die today."

Kamil glanced away at the utterance of *innocent*.

Their voice came out feeble and cracked and frozen: "I'm sorry."

"It isn't your fault."

They sniffed. Their lips split and the blood crystallized almost instantly. "It ... hurts. So much."

The vast emptiness in Friede's chest roiled. There was a time she felt the same, but it was buried and cold. She could not reach it. "You don't know what I would give to feel your pain. To hurt again. Trust me — you don't want this."

"It's all gone," they murmured. Their chin lowered to their chest, and they began to shudder with small, almost silent sobs. "How do you do it?"

"Live?"

Friede leaned close to block the snow that still fell, though it seemed to be slowing a bit. Maybe the sky had finally emptied itself. She said, "I didn't have a choice. So, I choose to feel everything I have left. The good and the ugly — it doesn't matter. Whatever makes it worth it to stay another day is a miracle. Can you do that? Can you get back to town, and stay one more day for me?" She offered them a hand.

"I'm sorry," Kamil said again, voice so small.

"I know. It's all right."

Snow gathered on her open palm, shreds of severed flesh and nerve. Friede thought of Bast's words and tried to find comfort there, enough to make an offering: "Lor's gone. She can't hurt us anymore."

Dark eyes flicked up, then down again. "Really gone?"

"Yes," Friede replied. She tried to smile through the bitter taste of the words. "She's paid the price." They could rejoice in that fact at least, and mourn the rest. Mourning was second nature.

Kamil didn't take her hand. They shrugged stiffly out of their soaked coat and into Friede's, still much too big for their frame. Frozen tears clung to their lashes like tiny pearls, shattering with each blink. Then they fit their fingers between the gaps left in hers, and an idea struck Friede as they stood together.

"Someone else will need to play the church's requiems now," she said, finding a strange peace in the words. "I could show you the details. You've already got the skill."

Kamil's eyes stared wide. "Me?"

"You're perfect," Friede said.

They cast her a long look and threw their arms out and embraced her. It lasted just a moment, but it made Friede's legs weak. She let herself briefly cradle the back of their head, savoring the rise and fall of their chest and the wispy whorls their breath made in the air.

"Follow my tracks back to town."

They looked so young when they answered, "What about you?"

Friede smiled; it was a small thing. "I'd just slow you down. I'll follow when I'm able. Please, go. Now. While you still can." She squeezed their hand as best she could.

Kamil worried their lip between their teeth, but nodded and pulled away. They didn't look back as they tramped off through the snow astride Friede's tracks, first slow and unsteady, then with increasing speed. The length of Friede's coat trailed behind them like an ill-fitting shadow.

"Tell Bastian I'm sorry, if you see him."

Friede had become so stiff she couldn't be sure if she actually spoke the words. Or if anyone heard her at all.

She watched until Kamil hurried over the hill and disappeared. Then she sat down in the snow as darkness crowded around her, and cast her gaze to the sky.

Gradually, the flakes petered out. Above, fat, dark clouds whirled like a riotous sea. She hoped for a glimpse of stars between them but found only black.

Friede imagined those far constellations, their impossible heat. Imagined it warming her, imagined sleeping for a long time. She was tired. Moreso in death than she'd ever been in life. Soul-tired. The weariness deep in her bones weighed her down, and Friede doubted she would stand again. She only wished she could have apologized to Bastian face to face, to beg him to forgive her for leaving him alone.

She would treasure one last word. Even if it was to refuse her. He deserved that chance, but she wasn't strong enough.

She bowed her head and let the sobs come. They started quietly, only shaking her shoulders a little, then it was like a storm breaking, and Friede couldn't help but let out a long cry. The sound carved her hollow on the way out.

She thought of Bast, and the sobs kept coming, breaking apart into screams. The residual heat of Kamil's embrace melted the snow in her hair and sent imitation tears down her face. Friede tried to blink them away, but her vision went dim. For a moment, she thought this must be it — cruel oblivion had come for her finally — but her consciousness never wavered. Her thoughts remained alert, many-edged. Grief still scratched, ravening, at the stony chambers of her heart.

Friede wiped at her cheeks. They came away streaked dark. In the faint, spotty light, she saw shining red and, impossibly, smelled the coppery tang of fresh blood. It was a scent one didn't forget.

Blood on her cheeks. On her hands, warm and wet. She blinked again and felt the same heat roll from her eyes.

They were her tears. Tears of blood.

Impossible, Friede thought, even as she tasted their sickening tang.

Before she could find her voice enough to cry out in shock or disgust, a great wind swirled about her, and Friede's head snapped back to see only black.

No stars. No night. Just black.

Great black wings.

CHAPTER FIFTEEN

THE END

The Pallwood's tangled trees were gone, the hills and clouds too. Before Friede spanned only pure white snow breaking against pitch sky. Her hands sat splayed open in her lap to catch the blood that fell from her eyes like summer rain. Drip, drip, drip. Disgustingly warm.

Perhaps this was the end, then.

Friede refused to shut her eyes. She would not give herself over to the temptation, the siren song of oblivion beckoning her to sleep.

Bast wasn't here. She didn't know whether Kamil had made it safely back. Whatever this was could not be the peace she'd prayed for.

Friede stared at the sky until those vast wings shifted and seized her in another gust. They unfolded from within with a deep thrumming noise, like a heartbeat, beating and beating until they revealed a colorless center: a figure wrapped in a thin white shroud. They descended from that dark and fluttering heart to the snow without a sound, feet bare.

In the gap where a face should have been, there was only darkness.

Of course. Their skull had been lost. First given, then taken, and hidden away somewhere she still did not know.

Friede found that she wasn't afraid.

A moment of awe flickered past, leaving only anger and confusion. It gave her the strength to stand and brush the snow from her legs, straighten her spine, and wipe her eyes.

She would meet Death on even footing, if this was to be her end.

They were thin and slight in their veils, a head shorter than Friede. So small for a creature so mythical. They watched her without eyes, a piercing attention radiating from that blackness.

Death swayed forward, the many layers of their shroud whispering over one another in a small chorus. When a pale white hand appeared from their sleeve and reached out to wipe at the blood on Friede's cheeks, she stood perfectly still. Their wings enveloped her in rushing shadow. Her chest felt like a wound inflamed, angry and unfamiliar. Nothing like what she'd once felt, what she'd wanted.

Friede caught Death's fingers before they reached her. She was surprised to find she had such strength left in her hands. The bone beneath their skin creaked and cut into her like ice cold marble. With her other hand, she pulled down the hood of the shroud.

Out of the darkness tumbled gray-blonde locks, framing a porcelain face.

Friede gasped and snatched her hand back.

"Eluned?"

The creature smiled placidly. Delicate crow's feet crinkled at the corners of their eyes. They were black as the sky, nothing like Eluned's original blue.

Two bottomless pits.

"My servant is known to you?" asked the imitation with Eluned's voice, her face, her lips.

But it could not be her. She lay dead in the catacombs; Friede had seen her, touched her, watched the decay taking its toll.

This was an insult.

Friede found her voice at last. The taste of blood sat heavy on her tongue, stuck between her teeth like stubborn weeds. "Her name is Eluned."

Death tilted their head, still smiling. "I know this," they said. The timbre was off. A low crackling undercut the words like a phonograph's rasp. They sounded hollow. "She is mine, in life and death. As are you."

Friede tried to back away, but Death's wings kept her tangled and pressed uncomfortably close. Eluned's pale hands caught hers and held fast. "Your music," they continued. "Sweet offerings you have given me, year after year. I have heard them all."

She stumbled back. "My music is for the dead, not you."

Death laughed. The sound rang sharply in the tight space, almost childish in its lightness. "The dead and I are one. Not all souls dwell with me, but each must pass through me for their rest."

Eluned's mouth opened wide, and Friede flinched as a cacophony of voices erupted in the confines of her skull, echoing Death's words. There were hundreds, thousands, even. Their harmony was uncanny. It was agony. Friede cried out, and more bloody tears fell from her eyes. She sagged in Death's arms, suddenly sapped of strength.

"Let me go," she pleaded in a whisper. "I hate you. You've taken everything from me."

Cold fingers stroked her cheek. "Then why did you call on me? You prayed over my servant, heralded her to me. You bound yourself in melody. You are mine, Friede Inkerman, as she was. My anchor," they crooned.

Panic clawed at her. Friede cast her eyes about for an escape. She found none. The thick snow kept her ankles pinned; Death ensnared her in their wings. She had nowhere to run.

She fisted her hands in their funeral garb. She'd played a requiem and spoken the rites over Eluned, but she was no cleric. All she'd wanted was to save an innocent soul. One soul, at least.

But then, when had Death ever been fair? They only bargained with the desolate and desperate.

Friede sobbed and beat her mangled hands against their chest, useless as it was. More pleas tangled around her tongue. The tears stained her sleeve, forming a crimson chain around her wrist.

This was Death, and she was their herald.

Friede fought for her voice and asked, "Is Eluned at peace? And the others — Julius Delvin, Lor Besson?" Her lips ran slick and red. "Do they rest?"

Death seemed to consider. "Peace is such a human design. Like war," they mused, eyes empty as the horizon. "They are as the flakes of snow. As the roots of the trees under winter's mantle. Unending. Part of the whole."

Friede paused to weigh the thought. Not long ago, even just at the beginning of this day, she would have given anything not to be afraid anymore. Not to grieve anymore. If Death had asked, she might have given her soul. But as they said, maybe there was no end, not even in death.

Death, for all their so-called gifts, did not love her. They didn't know her.

But she knew Death.

Friede straightened her spine and glanced to the sky. Perhaps there was time for one more miracle.

"Cairney needs an Anchoret," she said. "So do you. Otherwise, you lose them, all the souls they promised to you. And me too."

The creature was silent. Their pitch-black eyes pinned her in place.

"I'll do it. I'll go back and hallow Cairney again. If you make me a promise."

They answered slowly, the tendons in their jaw bowstring-tight. "What do you desire?"

Lor's words sprang to her mind.

I could have struck a better bargain.

Now was the time to ask, to resurrect that first terrible wish.

Friede couldn't do it. None of them should have ever bargained to begin with. And she wouldn't insult Lor's memory with another unburying. This refusal, too, was love.

"A year," Friede said. "I'll serve, be your Anchor for a year, so you can have your souls. And next Allhallowsmas, you'll find someone else. I'll have my eternal rest. Do we have a deal?"

The wind howled. Death's smile remained etched in porcelain. Their wings beat hard, tightening around her. "Yes."

At their word, the mantle of darkness tangled around them gave a shudder. It passed through the trees and into the ground. Friede's knees shook with its passing, but she stayed upright, gripping Death about the shoulders with only the strength of only her hate and love left.

"Where is your skull?" Friede demanded.

They turned and gazed into the faraway blankness of the sky, chin upturned as if scenting the air. Eluned's long hair lifted and swirled in the breeze. "It is where you and I first became one, Friede Inkerman."

Confusion flared in Friede's chest, then a lance of pain, of understanding.

She had been wrong, then.

Lor's last word to her had not been a refusal. The shape had seemed to be at first, to Friede's eyes — so clouded by anguish and the smoldering of her anger.

Her answer hadn't been *no,* but *home.*

Lor had tried to save her after all.

Friede wept hot, bloody tears in the stillness that followed. Then Death leaned forward, rising on air and wings to place a kiss on her chapped, bloody lips. The rushing wind came again, tearing at the edges of Friede's world until it succumbed to the darkness.

CHAPTER SIXTEEN

HEREAFTER

"Friede. *Friede.*"

She opened her eyes.

Bastian was above her, his face cast mostly in shadow and haloed by lacy snowflakes. He held her tight against his chest, one hand on her face, wiping at the crusting blood. She no longer felt its heat.

When her eyes found his, he made a beautiful sound, almost like a laugh. Despite her fatigue, Friede managed to raise her hand to stroke the ends of his curls that dangled over her. She could barely believe their softness.

"What happened?" he asked. "Whose blood is this?"

Behind him, streaks of violet colored the sky between the clouds.

With a lurch that broke apart the small layer of snow that coated her limbs, she rose up in his arms. She fisted her hands in the front of his cleric's robes and clung tightly. The smallest of smiles bloomed on her face, the same stiff, cold skin she knew so well.

"A miracle," she said without mirth.

Bast only stared. "How?"

She didn't know where to begin. The words poured out clotted and messy, her throat raw. "Death and I made a deal," she said. "I'm the Anchoret."

He scanned her face wildly. She felt half mad, and must have looked it too, but she hardly cared. She was back, and he'd come for her when she was unable to come back on her own. She didn't know why she had ever doubted that he would.

His mouth opened and closed, opened and closed. Finally, he said, "I thought you wanted to leave."

"I do. But I have to save your soul first."

She let her weight carry her forward until her forehead pressed against his, cold flesh to cold flesh. He cupped her cheek and smoothed her hair, staring back in wide-eyed wonder. She wrapped her arms around him. She could have stayed like that forever, suspended in the snow and holding him until they were nothing but anonymous bones. But it wasn't their time yet.

"I still don't forgive you," she said. "I think you took that from me."

"I know. I've loved you forever. I'll always love you. Here or there or hereafter or anywhere — wherever the fuck we go — doesn't matter."

Friede smiled. She wanted to kiss him, and realized at once that she'd wanted to for years. But if she gave in now, there was no telling when they'd stop. And she needed something to look forward to.

"We need to go," Friede said. But when she tried to stand, her knees buckled halfway, and she fell back into Bast's arms. She groaned and said again, "We need to go." But speaking the truth didn't conjure any strength in her frame. The wind blew at her back in beseeching gusts.

"All right. Just hold tight," Bast said.

He rose up, taking her weight with him. He lifted her into his arms as if she were nothing but a heap of twigs despite her height. "Where are we going?"

She rested her head in the curve of his clavicle. "The lake behind the house."

Bast nodded. More questions gleamed in his warm eyes, but he didn't speak them, simply took her on faith. Far steadier than he had any right to be, he started off marching for the hills, paling brow set in determination.

The woods seemed hungry to welcome them home. Even the snow seemed softer, more yielding in the wake of their return. They passed the old gnarled oak with its heart laid bare to the elements; black-winged vultures gathered in the skinny branches and snow below, busy at work on Lor's corpse. Friede didn't look. The Lor she'd known and loved and hated was gone. Cast far away in a place where she couldn't hurt, or be hurt in return, only mourned.

Friede clung to Bast's shoulders as they passed, fighting the urge to shut her eyes. She was so tired. But there was still work to be done. Eluned's work was unfinished. She wouldn't disappoint her.

The setting sun was as thin as a blade against the horizon when they descended the hill toward town. The distant lights of Cairney twinkled off the winding river, multiplied in the greenhouses of the garden district, warm and inviting.

Bast somehow found enough fortitude to hurry, and before long, they reached the cobbled streets awash with slush and ice. Friede didn't know if it was some trick of her mind, or something to do with the blood crusted on her cheeks, but she thought that if she focused, she could feel a faint pull in her chest and behind her eyes when she looked in the direction of the lake. Like the moon calling to the tide, its gravity tugged on the waterlogged places inside her; she was tethered now to that piece of Death.

Bast wove between the empty streets, his lurching steps reverberating in her bones like a song. Through scattered open windows, Friede heard music and prayers, laughter and children's voices. A town both alive and dead, built on grief's bones, carrying on the only way it knew how.

When they spilled out onto the street that bore her family home, Bast finally let her down. He wobbled on his feet when free of her weight. She wasn't much steadier, but she placed her riven hands over his, let his fingers fill in the gaps.

They walked to the edge of the lake together, the pull growing stronger with every step. Mud and moss sucked at their shoes; mist wafted from the dim greenish water and caressed her ankles. She sensed Death's eyes upon her from the dark bottom of the lake, anchoring her. She still heard Eluned's stolen voice in her skull, calling her down. A melody praying for an echo.

For once, Death called on her for help.

Friede had a strong urge to refuse them, to damn the town that had driven her to such lengths. She was heavy and tired, full of contradictions. Alive and dead; chosen by Death, and at the same time, she felt reviled by them. But Cairney needed her. Kamil needed her — so did Bast. And she needed him, but perhaps never more than this moment, when the fretted surface of the lake hissed at their feet. She felt its cold in her bones, paralyzing.

"Are you sure about this?" Bast asked. The house loomed over their heads like a gravestone. Friede's mettle wavered in its long shadow. She forced herself to nod.

"I can do it," he offered.

He was still trying to protect her. Nevermind that he'd carried her out from the jaws of oblivion twice now. It was her turn.

"I'm Death's chosen now. It has to be me." She smiled softly. "But you can hold my hand."

He nodded, as earnest as she'd ever seen him. "I've got you," he said, gripping her tightly. "I won't let you go."

She grasped him firmly back, looking into his mismatched eyes until her knees stopped shaking. Friede still wanted to kiss him. Where sour water and weeds had been before, the taste of that want lingered sweet in her throat, a familiar urge she'd forbidden herself from feeling a million times over. It tasted like a beginning and an ending all at once. Like a rebellion. Something even Death couldn't touch. And what a miracle that was.

She had a year to devise more rebellions. To decide what she was. A year to grieve, to hope, to love, to count her losses, of which she knew there would be many. But in this moment, Friede chose to hold tight to Bastian's hand and step into the murmuring water.

ACKNOWLEDGMENTS

Thank you to all the friends and loved ones who have encouraged my writing over the years leading to this book, and in no particular order: Tori Sharp, Perry Meester, Jeana Coppa. Thank you to my kind editor Anna Kubik for her attention and care, to Eden Holden for sensitivity reading, and Adele Edwards for beta reading and offering insightful feedback; you all made this book much better.

Thank you to Steve Wands and the entire team at Dead Sky Publishing who helped put this book out into the world, and Alex Eckman-Lawn for his stunning work on the cover art – working with you was a dream come true.

Thank you to my critique group on Discord for all your support and encouragement, and to anyone I've ever played D&D with; you helped me become a better storyteller.

I also want to thank author Paul Lisicki for his memoir *The Narrow Door*; hearing his words on grief gave me language for my own during one of the most difficult times of my life, when I needed them badly.

And to my mother Doreen, wherever she is now: every word of this book is for you. I was too broken to give you an honest eulogy when I had the chance, but I hope this book suffices as a replacement. Some days I forgive you and others I don't, but I love you all the same.

ABOUT THE AUTHOR

Carly is a writer, editor, and vulture enthusiast with a passion for the fantastical and visceral. She has a bachelor's degree in English with a concentration in creative writing from Arcadia University, and has written for a horror film festival and a TTRPG publisher. She currently works in social media marketing and serves as an editor for Luna Station Quarterly. Her work has appeared in Cosmic Horror Monthly, The NoSleep Podcast, NECKSNAP Magazine, and more. *Funeral Song* is her debut novella.

When she's not writing, Carly can be found drawing, watching horror movies, and playing video games or D&D, usually while drinking something caffeinated. She hopes to one day publish novels and write for a video game (or several). She can be found on most socials @willowylungs and at carlyracklin.com.